"You are no longer in Turkey, archaeologist."

The icy gray eyes of the man holding the rifle met Rose's steadily. "You have crossed the border. You are now within the sovereign territory of the Soviet Union."

There was an appalled silence. Rose stared at the hard, square-jawed face. The wind howled outside the cave.

"How could that happen?" she whispered, and he shrugged.

"In these mountains it is easy enough.... The weather is the more pressing problem. You have no firewood, and no food. You will either freeze or starve to death. You must come with me."

"But where—"

"Back into Turkey." He spoke patiently, but without warmth. "I myself will guide you. But remember this: alone, you would have died. You owe me your life, Englishwoman."

Books by Madeleine Ker

HARLEQUIN ROMANCES

2595—VOYAGE OF THE MISTRAL
2636—THE STREET OF THE FOUNTAIN

HARLEQUIN PRESENTS

642—AQUAMARINE
656—VIRTUOUS LADY
672—PACIFIC APHRODITE
699—THE WINGED LION

These books may be available at your local bookseller.

For a list of all titles currently available,
send your name and address to:

Harlequin Reader Service
P.O. Box 52040, Phoenix, AZ 85072-2040
Canadian address: P.O. Box 2800, Postal Station A,
5170 Yonge St., Willowdale, Ont. M2N 5T5

The Street of the Fountain

Madeleine Ker

Harlequin Books

TORONTO • NEW YORK • LONDON
AMSTERDAM • PARIS • SYDNEY • HAMBURG
STOCKHOLM • ATHENS • TOKYO • MILAN

Original hardcover edition published in 1984
by Mills & Boon Limited

ISBN 0-373-02636-6

Harlequin Romance first edition August 1984

Printed in U.S.A.

CHAPTER ONE

THE snow whirled in dense sheets in front of the mouth of the cave. Outside, Rose knew, the whole landscape would be blanketed in white by now. The savage, rocky terrain of Agri, the easternmost province of Turkey, would have disappeared under the kindly mantle of death. She drew the rough coat closer around her shoulders, and shivered. The fire which Azdhani had managed to make from twigs was giving out only the barest amount of warmth. For the first time, it began to occur to her that her situation might be serious. She looked up at the old man, who was methodically stuffing his pipe.

'Azdhani, how long will the snow last?'

Absorbed in his pipe, the old man puffed for a while, then shrugged.

'Who knows? Maybe a few hours. Maybe a week.'

'*A week?*' Considerably dampened, Rose turned to glance at the saddlebags which they had piled at the back of the cave. They had bargained on staying away from the camp for a maximum of five days. And they had already consumed three days' worth of their supplies. Azdhani puffed on impassively. The two donkeys, who had lain down beside them on the rocky floor of the cave, stared out at the snow with patient brown eyes.

'Will they send out a search-party for us?'

The old man shook his head.

'It is too dangerous in the snow. The animals would not be able to see the rocks—they would stumble and fall.'

'Couldn't they send a helicopter from Erzerum?'

Rose suggested anxiously. For answer, Azdhani pointed to the heavy, dark clouds which were rolling only a few hundred feet above the cave, completely obscuring the mountain peaks. It was obviously impossible for any helicopter to attempt to penetrate the snowstorm.

'It is far better to wait,' the old man said. His wise old eyes took Rose's anxious expression in, and he smiled. 'We will be fine, Miss Johnson. It was indeed providential that we found this cave. Allah be praised,' he added softly, and resumed his pipe.

The heavy smell of the Turkish tobacco comforted her slightly; the old man seemed untroubled by their predicament. Why should she worry?

'All right,' she sighed, and rummaged in the saddlebags for the little tin kettle.

By the time the tea had brewed, the light was beginning to fade. There was no sign of the snow abating; it continued to whirl down in silent curtains. Rose sipped the scalding brew gratefully. The rough Armenian coat she was wearing, which had at first seemed to her like an old Turkish rug with a hole in the middle, was surprisingly warm. Thank God she hadn't left it behind! She pulled the hood up to cover her head. The autumn snows, it seemed, had come early this year.

The expedition had been her own idea. After three months on the archaeological dig at Igdir, Rose had grown tired of the endless vista of trenches and mounds of dark earth. When the director of the excavation, Selman Hristaki, had mentioned the ruins at Ispir, Rose had pricked up her ears. Ispir was a good sixty miles from the camp, and in the remotest countryside, near the Armenian border—but all that suited Rose equally well. After all, she had come to Turkey for solitude. And instead of solitude at Igdir, she had found herself cooped up at close quarters with an international community of archaeologists, led by the smiling Professor Hristaki, of Istanbul University. Far from peace and quiet, Rose had found her days filled with painstaking work, her leisure hours filled with the noisy company of the archaeological team.

Not that she minded them—they were a cheerful, convivial enough bunch. It was just that conviviality was the last thing she had wanted. She had wanted solitude, silence. Silence in which to get over Barry.

At the beginning of October, in less than ten days, the dig was due to close for the winter—and then she was going to be at a loose end again. She realised that she had seen almost nothing of this part of Turkey apart from the monotonous trenches at the excavation. Suddenly, she had wanted to see something else before the season ended.

The old man rose, interrupting her thoughts, and began to prepare rice for their evening meal.

'How far are we from the ruins, Azdhani?' she asked.

'Not more than a few miles,' the old man told her. 'Perhaps the snow will be gone by tomorrow, and we will be able to continue.' He went on with the preparations in silence. They both knew that the chances of the snow being gone by morning were very slight. When Rose had asked Professor Hristaki for permission to visit the ruins at Ispir, the September skies had been blue and clear. This heavy snow had appeared with the suddenness of a pouncing animal, an icy, deadly creature that had come straight down from Moscow.

Which reminded her that the Soviet border was barely a day's ride from where they now sat, blanketed in snow. Just before the snow had come, the old guide had pointed laconically at the long line of dark mountains that extended towards Mount Ararat in the South.

'Russia,' he had said simply. And she had shivered. Now she shivered again.

Nor did it escape her, when Azdhani dished up their supper of rice and beans, that the old man had given them very small portions indeed. He was clearly anticipating a long wait in the cave—and their rations would have to be scrupulously conserved. She ate in silence, aware that the bowlful of unappetising stew wasn't going to satisfy her ravenous hunger to any appreciable extent. The donkeys watched them eat with soft eyes. There would be no supper for them tonight; the coarse grass, so abundant in these rocky hills, was buried in the snow. When they had eaten, Rose curled up against the warm flank of Suleiman, her own donkey, and stared into the flickering embers of Azdhani's fire. Well, she now had what she wanted—the isolation she had craved for, and a chance to sort out her inner feelings.

Barry Morrison had been the handsomest man Rose had ever set eyes on. With his willowy figure, and that angelic combination of fair hair and blue eyes, he had smitten more hearts than one at college. He had possessed an elusive, almost girlish charm, which seemed to fascinate women. They longed to smooth those golden curls, to mother him, to satisfy that worried look that always hovered on his heavy lids. He was adorable, they had all agreed.

But to Rose he was more—much more. He had been her first love, her only love, the man in whom she had placed all her trust and confidence. She had scarcely believed her luck when Barry had reciprocated her feelings for him; and the eight months of their engagement had been the happiest, the most glorious period of a life which had been generally lonely and dull.

With a murmured goodnight, the old guide pulled his long cloak around himself, and curled up against the belly of the other donkey, which sighed as expressively as a human being before closing its own long-lashed eyes. In the silence, broken only by the crackles of the fire and the almost inaudible rustle of the snow, Rose Johnson reflected bitterly on the brevity of man's love.

Would Barry ever know how much he had hurt her? And why was it that one only realised the truth about people when it was too late? Because it was only while Barry had actually been explaining to her why their engagement had to be cancelled that Rose had realised that the Barry Morrison she had loved so passionately was a figment of her own imagination. The casual boy who had thrown her over for another woman had never reciprocated her feelings. Barry Morrison, in fact, was incapable of ever feeling the depth of emotion which Rose had known for those wonderful, terrible eight months.

Disbelief had numbed the pain for a few days. She had expected Barry to return daily, to explain that it had all been a terrible mistake, or a cruel joke.

And then it had dawned on her at last. He wasn't coming back. She had lost him.

She had never had him in the first place.

The snow whirled at the entrance to the cave, dancing in the bitterly cold air in ever-thicker sheets. The great snow-monster was gathering, from Archangel in the immensity of the north, down over Moscow, Tambov, Volgagrad, across the towering fangs of Georgia, and into eastern Turkey, more than fifteen hundred miles to the south. Rose stared with unseeing brown eyes at the whirling darkness. In all that coldness, she thought bitterly, there was nothing to match the coldness in her own heart.

Never again. She had sworn it on the ashes of her passion for Barry. Never again would she surrender all to any man, never would she give her heart again.

From now on, any relationships she entered would be strictly on her own terms. And that meant personal freedom. No commitments. Not an inch given or asked for.

And never again that empty, cynical charade called love.

The fire flickered out soon after she had drifted into sleep, and she awoke in the early hours of the morning, shivering with cold. It was pitch black, and the snow was still rustling down outside. Rose snuggled closer against the donkey's furry flank, trying to share the patient creature's body-warmth. Poor Suleiman! His stomach would be emptier than hers. She reached out in the darkness, and rubbed the velvety muzzle. Suleiman replied with a half-hearted lick, then grunted, stretching out his short legs. She pulled the rough coat over her frozen nose and allowed herself to drift back into an uncomfortable sleep.

Morning dawned dim and icy. She awoke with a start, her hands and face icy cold. The cave was half full of snow, and lit with a frozen grey light. Azdhani had built another tiny fire from the remainder of the dry twigs that lay on the cave's floor, and was stirring a billy-can of porridge on the embers. The snow was still pouring down.

''Morning, Azdhani.' Rose struggled to her feet, combing her long chestnut hair into some semblance of order with her fingers.

'Good morning, Miss Johnson.' The old man gestured with his spoon at the drifting snow. 'It has not stopped yet. I fear that we shall be confined here for some time.' He looked up at her from under shaggy eyebrows. 'Perhaps several days.'

'Oh,' she said dismally. 'Have we enough food to last that long?'

'Firewood is our more immediate concern,' Azdhani

smiled. His lined, intelligent face, weathered by the years into the colour of old mahogany, was fatalistic. 'It will be very difficult to find fuel in the snow. But as for food——' He waved a gnarled hand at the two donkeys, grinned, then started dishing the porridge up. Rose felt physically sick. The thought of killing and eating her faithful donkey revolted her inexpressibly. She would sooner starve, she resolved, than descend to eating poor Suleiman. Why, it would be like cannibalism!

She accepted the bowl from Azdhani, and spooned the lukewarm gruel down with relish. Tasteless as it was, it would supply the essential calories that would keep her warm—warm and alive—for the next few hours.

Really, she had been very foolish. Why on earth had she insisted on going alone? Indeed, she would have set off without Azdhani, had not Selman Hristaki insisted that she take a guide. There were several of the others who had wanted to come—especially Tom Lewis, the senior archaeologist, who was showing every sign of romantic interest in Rose; but she had insisted almost violently that she wanted to go alone. Professor Hristaki, she suspected, had given private instructions to the others to let her be. He at least had understood her craving for peace and solitude.

'Nevertheless,' he had warned her, his black eyes sympathetic, 'you must take Azdhani with you. You could easily get lost up in the hills—the road is a very poor one. Besides which, it's not unknown for Armenian bandits to cross the border—and I would hate anything to happen to you up there.' Rose glanced at the curved knife hanging at the old man's side, and smiled to herself. Azdhani must be seventy at least; what protection would he be? Professor's Hristaki's talk of bandits, she was sure, had been a bit of local colour thrown in to make her see the sense of taking the old guide with her. Well, thank goodness she had agreed. The old man puffed at his pipe peacefully, staring out at the whirling snow. There seemed to be an abundant supply, at least, of his tobacco. It was very rare to meet a Turk who did not smoke, in this land of cheap, fragrant tobacco. The yellow stains on Azdhani's fierce white moustache bore witness to a lifetime's smoking; nor did he seem to be any the less robust for the habit. Azdhani was one of the lucky ones.

Out of sheer habit, Rose fished the little hand-mirror out of her shoulder-bag, and began to rub cream into her chapped lips and cheeks. The face that looked back at her was almost a perfect oval, with wide, velvet-lashed brown eyes, a straight nose, and a full mouth that, if it were not so chapped and pinched with cold, would be satin-skinned and soft. It was a vulnerable, attractive face, a face that reflected its owner's emotions all too readily.

Straightening up, Rose realized with dismay that the icy cold was creeping insidiously into her limbs. Her joints felt stiff, the bones beginning to ache unpleasantly. Catching her grimace, Azdhani nodded. Coming over to her, he pulled the hood of her coat up to keep her face warm, and tied the knot under her chin.

'The cold is our worst enemy,' he said seriously. 'If we do not keep ourselves warm, we shall simply drift into a long sleep. And then into the longest sleep of all. We must keep moving.' A mischievous glint came into his wrinkled eyes. 'We shall have to play street games, like children. Have you ever seen the children play *kayiçi* in Stamboul?'

'I don't think so,' she smiled. 'But I'm willing to learn.'

'Good.' The old guide scrambled to his feet. 'It's very simple—we have to pretend that we are fishermen in a boat, and as we row ourselves along, we sing these words—we have to sit down, like this——'

Within minutes they were both convulsed with laughter as they rocked to and fro next to the fire, chanting the nonsense-words together. Azdhani took the part of the grumpy old fisherman, Rose mewing out the lines of the wicked cat who tried to steal his catch. They were chanting out the chorus with gusto when the words suddenly froze in the old man's throat. His eyes widened in alarm as he stared over Rose's shoulder to the entrance of the cave. Her heart leaping, she spun round, dropping Azdhani's gnarled hands—and with cold shock, found herself staring down the muzzle of a rifle.

The man holding the weapon stared at them both in astonishment for a long second, his eyes flicking from one to the other; and then, shaking the snow from his furs, he advanced into the cave. But he did not put down the rifle; and his eyes remained the coldest grey Rose had ever seen. She and Azdhani sat immobile with shock as he surveyed them from under lowered brows. Suddenly, Selman Hristaki's talk of Armenian bandits did not seem fanciful at all. A chill fragment of fear stabbed her heart.

Ignoring Rose, the stranger turned to the old man and barked out a question in Turkish. As the old man stammered out a reply, she studied him covertly. He was tall and broad, but so muffled in a heavy fur jacket that she could distinguish nothing of his figure. His face, as far as she could see it under the fur hood he wore, was aquiline, savage; a three or four-day stubble of beard covered his cheeks, and the cold grey eyes were bleak. He was as savage and wild an apparition as could have sprung from this wilderness of snow and rock; yet she found time to notice that the boots he wore were supple and finely made—and the rifle that pointed with unwavering steadiness between them was modern, and gleaming with oil.

Having considered the old man's reply, the stranger flicked his eyes back to Rose's face. A shiver went through her very soul as she met the hard, bright gaze that surveyed her face.

'So,' he said abruptly, his voice deep and carrying a trace of accent, 'the old man says you are an English archaeologist. Is this true?'

'Yes,' she nodded, then swallowed to ease the tightness in her throat. 'We were heading for the ruins at Ispir when we——'

'Where are you based?' he interrupted coldly.

'At Igdir. I'm part of the international dig there.' Suddenly conscious of the indignity of her position on the cold floor, she scrambled to her feet. The old man tried to lay a restraining hand on her sleeve, but it was too late. The muzzle of the rifle thudded with breath-robbing force into her midriff.

With a gasp of pain, she collapsed back on to the rock. Her hood slid back, releasing her long, chestnut hair, which tumbled in glossy profusion around her face.

The icy grey eyes widened in surprise at the sight of the pale, oval face that stared up at him, blurry-eyed with tears.

'A girl!' he said sharply, and for the first time seemed to hesitate. 'I could not see your face under that hood,' he informed her. And as though underlining the fact that that wasn't an apology, his gloved hands raised the rifle again, and cocked it. The metallic clicks were horrifyingly loud in the confined space of the cave.

'If you move again,' he said quietly, 'I will shoot you.'

Mute with pain, anger and fear, Rose did not even stir to wipe the tears that had trickled scaldingly down her cheeks. The old man let out his breath with a sigh, and murmured something in Turkish, obviously trying to conciliate the stranger. Ignoring his words, the man kept his icy grey eyes fixed on Rose.

'If you were travelling from Igdir to Ispir, what are you doing here?' he rasped.

'I tried to tell you,' she gritted out, the pain in her solar plexus still cruel. 'We were caught by the snow, and we had to take shelter in this cave. We're only a few miles from the ruins, but——'

'A few miles?' The grey eyes flicked back to the old man. 'Do you expect me to believe such a childish deception?'

'You have no reason to disbelieve us,' Rose retorted angrily. 'We've done no harm! Why are you treating us as though we were criminals?'

'Criminals?' The cold eyes sneered. 'You are either criminals or fools, that is certain.' He considered them both for a few seconds, then gestured with his rifle at the saddlebags that lay next to the quietly watching donkeys. 'You,' he commanded the old man, 'open them.'

'I see,' Rose said softly, as the old man scrambled to obey him. 'That's what you came for, is it? To rob us?'

'Miss Johnson,' hissed the old man in an agony of anxiety, 'pray hold your tongue!'

'You would both do well to keep silent,' the stranger remarked in his deep, quiet voice. Thoughtfully, he studied the pile of belongings that Azdhani was hauling out of the saddlebags—food, spare clothing, Rose's camera and lenses, the few books on archaeology she had brought along.

'The books are worth nothing,' she said coldly. 'But doubtless you will get a few *lire* for the camera.' She met his eyes bravely—and thought she saw a hint of cruel amusement in the diamond-bright eyes. He looked from Rose to the old guide, who was standing respectfully next to the heap of their belongings, then he uncocked his rifle and laid it against the wall of the cave. Despite herself, Rose could not suppress a great sigh of relief, and the hint of amusement in his eyes became an icy little smile.

'You are such a pair of fools,' he remarked calmly, throwing back his hood, 'that I am almost tempted to believe you.' The face that was revealed was, she had to admit, intriguing. Beneath the beard, the hard lines of jawline and cheekbones were elegant and clear, and the sardonic mouth held a hint of restrained passion. The amusement, however, did not extend to his level eyes. Moving with silent grace, he squatted by the fire, and inspected the contents of the teapot that Azdhani had left there.

'Would you like some tea, *effendi*?' the old man offered hastily.

'Yes—I'm half frozen,' the stranger nodded curtly. As the old man busied himself with the billycan, the stranger watched him carefully.

'Are you really such an idiot as you look, old man?'

'*Effendi?*'

The man took up the map that had been lying next to him, and folded it out under Azdhani's startled nose.

'Show me where we are,' he commanded.

'Here, *effendi*,' the old guide said with dignity, putting his wizened finger on a spot near Mount Ararat.

'So?' The grey eyes met Rose's. 'You agree with him, archaeologist?'

She shrugged bitterly. 'Why should I doubt him?'

He stared at her a moment longer, then nodded absently.

'Indeed, it is as I supposed. You are nothing more than a pair of fools.'

'You can check with Professor Hristaki at Igdir if

you doubt us,' Rose retorted angrily. 'Though I don't see that you have any right to!'

'I shall certainly check,' the stranger nodded with a bleak smile. 'And it will go very hard with both of you if I find that you have lied.'

'What right have you to talk like this?' she snapped suddenly.

'Miss Johnson——' began the old man anxiously, but Rose ignored him; she had lost patience with this cold, brutal man and his sneering words.

'We have as much right to be here as you do, whatever we are. Turkey is a free country, you know!'

'Indeed,' the other murmured, pulling off his gloves, and warming his strong hands at the fire. 'But you are no longer in Turkey, archaeologist.'

'*What?*'

The old man froze, and looked up with fearful eyes.

'You have crossed the Russian border, archaeologist. You are now fives miles within the sovereign territory of the Soviet Union.'

There was an appalled silence. Rose's jaw dropped open, then she turned to Azdhani in incomprehension.

'But—but—how could that have happened?'

'At the pass,' the old man groaned in misery. 'I must have taken the wrong turning at the pass. It is so many years since I travelled this route! I had my doubts at the time—I——'

The stranger took the billycan from the old man's nerveless fingers.

'Perhaps you should have retired years ago,' he suggested drily, stirring in a spoonful of green tea.

'But you must understand that this has all been a terrible mistake,' Rose blurted out. 'We had no intention of trespassing on Russian soil!'

'*Effendi*,' the old man quavered. 'she is right. As soon as the *effendi* pleases, we shall return back to Turkish soil——'

'The matter is not so simple as you seem to think,' the tall man said softly. Rose stared at the hard, square-jawed face, and noticed for the first time that the black hair, flecked with grey at the temples, was cut short. As short as a military officer's. 'You have chosen to take shelter,' he pursued, 'barely three miles from Yerevan. Which,' he informed them, pouring himself a cup of tea, and watching them with ruthless amusement over the rim of his cup, 'happens to be the most secret military base in this whole region.'

Azdhani groaned, tugging at his white moustache.

'Believe us, *effendi*,' he said urgently, 'we are not Western spies. We saw nothing of the base—we did not even know it was there——'

'The old man is right,' said Rose, twisting her hands nervously. 'Surely you wouldn't dream of taking reprisals against two innocent sightseers——'

'Reprisals?' the man repeated, raising an eyebrow in an arc of dry amusement. 'My dear archaeologist, you seem to think that Russians are monsters!'

There was an embarrassed silence.

'I didn't mean——' Rose began, but he cut her short.

'The weather is a more pressing problem at the moment,' he said calmly. 'The snow is going to keep falling for many days yet. Which means that the passes are going to be deep in drifts.' His sharp gaze raked the cavern. 'You have no firewood, very little food. You will either starve to death or freeze within a few days. You cannot stay here.'

'But where can we go, *effendi*?' the old man pleaded. 'I am no longer young—I could not go far in this weather——' He gestured helplessly at the whirling snow outside.

'Couldn't—couldn't you call for some of your men to pick us up?' Rose suggested tentatively.

'My men? What men?' The freezing grey eyes silenced her for a second, then she looked away.

'Your soldiers,' she clarified. 'Aren't you stationed at this place—what's it called, Yerevan?'

'No,' he said curtly. 'And there is no question of sending Russian soldiers to help you. That would place this whole foolish episode on an official level. You understand? You would have to be taken to Yerevan, interrogated.'

Somehow, the word sent a shiver through both Rose and Azdhani, and they looked at one another in dismay.

'No doubt,' the other shrugged, 'you would be sent back in time—but a most embarrassing diplomatic incident might be precipitated. It is unfortunate for you that you have chosen to trespass on a Soviet missile base. No,' he said decisively, tossing the dregs of his tea into the fire with a sharp hiss, 'there is no question of alerting the officials at Yerevan.' He surveyed them grimly. 'The best course will be to get you back across the Turkish border as soon as possible. Understood?'

'But——'

'Otherwise,' he said incisively, 'my position will be most embarrassing. I should have to take an official stance on this matter. And you and your elderly friend would have to spend many weeks in an Armenian prison.' They digested this in silence, as he watched them with clever, cold eyes. Azdhani spread his hands in an age-old gesture of resignation.

'The officer is right, Miss Johnson. It is really very kind of him to take so lenient a view of our error.'

Creep, creep, crawl, Rose thought bitterly; but seeing the real fear in Azdhani's eyes, she relented. To the Turks who lived on the Russian border, she knew, the Red Army was a terrifying presence. They were prone to regard Russians with an almost superstitious dread. The officer's talk of prison had shaken the old man badly.

'Well,' she said tightly, looking at the lean, aggressive face before her, 'it seems we have no choice but to put ourselves in your hands, Mr——'

The man ignored her probe after his name, and rose to his feet in one lithe movement.

'We will set off immediately,' he said in a clipped voice. The voice of a man to whom command and authority had become second nature. He slung the rifle over his shoulder, and watched impassively as they packed the saddlebags and tried to stir the donkeys into movement. The animals shuffled resentfully on frozen limbs, and Rose bit back her murderous anger against the callous way in which the Russian was behaving. If this was a specimen of Red Army hospitality, she thought furiously, they could keep it. When she got back to Igdir, she was jolly well going to raise a stink about this. Diplomatic incident! She was going to make a diplomatic incident all right!

The snow whipped at their faces with freezing claws as she and the old man stumbled out after the Russian officer. In the blizzard, it was almost impossible to tell where they were—they could see nothing but a white wilderness all around them. The Russian turned to look back, his grey eyes burning in the darkness of his hood like a wolf's.

'Stay close to me,' he barked into the wind. 'Understand?'

Rose nodded, clinging to the neck of Suleiman, who had begun to bray indignantly at the storm. Azdhani clambered on to the back of his donkey, the snow gathering in his grizzled moustache. Slowly, the little convoy set off into the raging blizzard.

Rose never knew how many hours they struggled

through the raging snow; she was soon numbed and exhausted. But towards the end of the day, the snow began to lift a little. Staring about her with tired eyes, she saw that they had come to the pass that led directly on to the road back to Igdir. Azdhani, clinging to his donkey's neck, nodded wearily.

'I know the way back now, *effendi*. Many thanks.'

'Go safely,' the Russian nodded, and smiled tightly at Rose. 'Do not stray from the fold again, little archaeologist—there are many wolves in these hills.' The pain in her midriff where his rifle-barrel had struck her had settled into a dull ache, and she was scarcely in the most cheerful of tempers. She glowered at him.

'I hope you're satisfied now, General,' she said sourly. 'We've saved you from your embarrassment.'

'And I have saved both your lives,' he replied calmly, his eyes boring into hers.

'We would have been perfectly all right without you,' she retorted.

'Without me you would have died, Englishwoman. You owe me a life.' With a harsh smile, he turned on his heel, and strode back towards the hills, the snow whirling around his tall, dark figure. She watched him until he disappeared, then muttered an unladylike epithet. Azdhani was staring about him, rubbing his chapped cheek in thought.

'Come on,' she said impatiently, 'let's get going.'

'At once, Miss Johnson,' he agreed, but did not move. 'Strange,' he muttered, staring at the pass, 'I could have sworn we took the right direction . . .'

'Well, we didn't,' Rose said drily. 'It was an easy mistake to make, Azdhani. Don't worry about it.'

'Indeed, as you say, Miss Johnson.' Slowly they led their donkeys down into the pass. The old man pointed to a snow-clad hill ahead. 'There is a shepherd's hut there. We'll spend the night there, then try to reach Igdir next day.' She nodded her agreement, too tired to talk. But as they trudged through the snow, Azdhani was shaking his head in puzzlement.

'Strange,' he was murmuring. 'Most strange.'

CHAPTER TWO

THEIR homecoming was satisfactorily dramatic. Professor Hristaki was so relieved to see them back safe despite the snow that he embraced them both like prodigal children, and within minutes of their arrival they were defrosting in front of the fire in the Professor's bungalow, one of the few permanent structures on the site, drinking *raki*. He listened to their tale with his usual smile in place; but when they had finished, his sloe-dark eyes were thoughtful.

I find it hard to believe you could have crossed the Russian border without knowing it,' he commented. 'It's very well signposted.'

Rose stopped towelling her abundant hair for a minute, and looked up at him. He surveyed her tousled, pretty face with a grave smile. 'But in the snow, of course,' he added, 'anything is possible.'

'Yet we saw no signposts or fences,' Azdhani mused. 'And I was utterly convinced that we were on the right path. There was something else, too . . .'

'What?' Rose demanded.

'That man—he did not seem to me like a Russian. He was not wearing the uniform of the Red Army, for one thing. And for another, the rifle he was holding was a hunter's weapon, not a soldier's.'

Grimacing at the memory, Rose rubbed her bruised midriff thoughtfully.

'But he said he came from the missile base at Yerevan,' she said.

The Professor shook his head.

'Yerevan?' he repeated. 'There is no missile base at

Yerevan, Rose. It is just a town, like any other.'

'What? Isn't it a top-secret missile base?'

'Hardly. And even if it were, the Russians would scarcely tell us about it.'

Rose and Azdhani stared at one another. Fury had began to settle in Rose's heart.

'We've been led up the creek,' she said to the old man. 'We were never in Russia at all!'

'I think you are right,' the guide agreed thoughtfully. He tossed off his *raki*. 'The more I think about it, the more obvious it seems to me. We couldn't possibly have crossed the border; we were exactly where we thought we were.'

'That swine!' Rose hissed, the memory of his callous blow rising before her eyes again. 'He wasn't a Russian soldier at all! For heaven's sake, what a pair of fools we were, Azdhani. Why did we let him bully us like that?'

'It is difficult to argue with *force majeure*,' the old man reminded her drily. 'With that rifle, he could have killed us both, and buried us in the snow. Whoever he was, we did well to obey him.'

'Azdhani is right,' Selman Hristaki agreed. 'Well, my dear Rose, you have at least had an adventure.'

'Adventure be damned!' she retorted angrily. 'He behaved abominably! We must tell the police at once, Professor.'

'Of course,' he soothed. 'Though they will have difficulty in finding your hero, whoever he is, in this weather.'

'He's not my hero,' she snapped. 'He assaulted me with a loaded rifle!'

'Yet it seems to me he saved your lives,' the Professor reminded her mildly, then lifted a slender hand to restrain her protestations. 'Anyway, let's discuss the whole thing tomorrow, my dear. At the moment, what you need is a hot bath—and then a good night's sleep. In the morning you will see the whole episode with a little more of your usual good humour!'

Strangely enough, though, Rose's usual good humour refused to reassert itself, even after a good night's sleep. A ball of resentment and anger seemed to have lodged itself in her gullet, and would not go away. There was something about the way the man had treated her—not just the way he had knocked her flat, but the icy contempt in his eyes, the silky irony in his deep voice—which haunted her. Through the next few days of patient work in the snow—the dig was not due to stop for another week yet—she found herself dwelling on the ruthless ease with which the Russian (she still called him that, mentally) had sent them scuttling home again.

The general consensus of opinion at the camp was that he must have been an Armenian bandit who had crossed the border for some purpose. Seeing that Rose and Azdhani had nothing worth stealing, they reasoned, he had taken pity on them, and had shepherded them home again. Even Azdhani inclined to this opinion; but Rose could not agree.

For one thing, the Russian had not looked or talked like a bandit. For all his savage appearance, the deep voice had been cultivated, urbane. She recalled the beautiful, expensive boots; and the hands she had watched him warming at the fire were strong but elegant—and far too well manicured for a bandit.

There was also the question of his lie about their having crossed the Soviet border.

'Why would he spin such a complicated tale?' Rose had demanded. 'It wasn't necessary.'

'Perhaps he simply wanted to scare you into moving more quickly?' Tom Lewis suggested.

'Yes,' Rose said decisively. 'He knew exactly what he was doing, Tom. He wanted us out of that area for some reason. It's my bet he was up to some skulduggery around there—drug-smuggling, probably. Or gun-running to the Kurds.'

Tom's sceptical smile left her unmoved. The Russian had been up to something around Ispir—of that she was certain—and she had said as much to the police constable from Tuzluca who called to take down the details of her complaint. He had treated her with the exquisite politeness which Turks reserve for foreigners—especially mad ones—and had obviously not believed a word of her tale.

'There are sometimes hunters in those parts,' he had suggested gently. 'Wild men—but they would do you no harm. And after all, did he not save your life?'

'He nearly shot me,' she retorted, and hoisted up her layers of sweaters and cardigans to show the young policeman the bruise across the silky skin of her stomach. Modestly, the constable averted his gaze from such an embarrassing exposure of foreign, female flesh, and had agreed reluctantly to convey her complaint to his chief in Tuzluca.

Which did not lessen Rose's indignation.

The winter was approaching fast, and work on the dig was due to cease at the beginning of October. There was an air of finality at Igdir. The last finds were being cleaned and catalogued, the trenches and pits covered over until the spring. There was much to do, though that didn't stop Rose from seething inwardly every time she thought back on the Russian's behaviour. How he must have laughed at them, the swine! They had been like putty in his strong brown hands, only too willing to obey that iron will. If she ever saw him again, she swore, she would tell him exactly what she thought of him!

Had she paused to consider, she would have been surprised to realise that, for the first time since Barry

Morrison had walked out on her, Rose Johnson was thinking long and hard about another man.

'It's been a good dig.' Tom Lewis drew deep on his cigarette, then flicked the butt into the snow. He and Rose were standing under the lean-to that served as the archaeologists' canteen, watching the sun set dimly in the west. He looked at her with thoughtful green eyes, rubbing his hand through his curly brown hair in a characteristic gesture. 'What will you do now, Rose?' he asked quietly.

'I'm not sure,' she confessed. 'Go back to Europe, I suppose. Maybe do a little sightseeing first.'

'You haven't got any family, have you?' he probed gently.

She shook her head.

'Just Freddie—my brother. He's in the States right now, working at a big hospital in Chicago. We don't have any parents.'

Tom nodded, then nervously lit another cigarette. Rose turned to him with a reproving smile, her deep brown eyes soft. 'You shouldn't smoke so many of those things, Tom.'

'I know, I know.' He smiled at her, then bit his lip. 'Look, Rose—I don't want to beat about the bush, because we've got so little time. The thing is—well, in a few days I'm going back to Australia. I've got a cottage on the beach near Bondi—miles of white sand and blue sky. And I'd like you to come and share it with me.' Rose looked up, and Tom waved his hand. 'Don't get me wrong, Rose—I don't mean anything physical, not if you don't want to. I've just—well, I've got to like your company, that's all.'

She looked back at the sunset, her mind troubled. It had not escaped her that Tom Lewis had, over the three months they had worked together, fallen slightly in love with her. She liked him well enough; he was a slight, nervous man, with thin, artistic hands and a diffident manner—quite unlike the stereotype of the burly, self-confident Aussie. Insofar as she could like or trust any man after what Barry had done to her, she liked Tom. A lot.

'Oh, Tom,' she sighed, 'that's so kind of you, but——'

'You don't have to give me your answer right away,' he said quickly, forestalling her refusal. 'I realise that you're still pretty mixed up inside.'

'That's very perceptive of you,' she said slowly. 'I didn't realise it showed.'

'Maybe it only shows to me,' he smiled, and inhaled a lungful of blue smoke, his eyes speculative. 'You came here with a personal devil on your tail, didn't you?'

'Something like that,' she agreed reluctantly.

'I don't want to know the details,' Tom said quietly. 'I presume some feller hurt you—more fool him. Of course, that's none of my business. But I can tell you're still thinking about him. That's why you came here, isn't it? To try and forget him?'

'Something like that,' she said again, staring into the soft Turkish darkness.

'Why did you choose this dig?' he asked.

'Because archaeology's one of the few things I know. Because I thought eastern Turkey would be remote enough to give me the solitude I needed.'

'Instead of which, you found yourself pestered by a nosy Aussie, eh?'

'You know that isn't true, Tom,' she smiled. 'I like you very much.'

'I like you, Rose. I like you a great deal.' He drew on his cigarette again, and the coal glowed in the near-darkness like a ruby. 'There's plenty of peace and quiet at Carnarvon Beach, Rose. You could just laze around all day, sunbathe, fish. I could teach you to surf, if you liked.'

'Tom——'

'It's a beautiful place, Rose. And you could stay as long as you liked, you know that.'

'Tom, you're so sweet,' she said, moved. 'But it wouldn't be fair to you if I came. You were right about my reason for coming here. Someone did hurt me. And I'm still trying to get over it.' She drew a deep breath. 'It happened during the last year of my archaeology course at college. I was very lucky to pass the exams. But I did—and when I saw the ad for this dig in *The Archaeologist*, it sounded like the very thing I needed.' She smiled softly at Tom in the darkness, though he couldn't see her face. 'Trouble is,' she whispered, 'it hasn't done the trick. I'm sorry, truly sorry. It's not you—I just couldn't trust myself with any man right now. And I don't think I could handle any kind of relationship—even the sort of friendship you've suggested. I don't think that would satisfy you, either,' she added.

And who knows, she thought with inward stab of bitterness, maybe even you, gentle Tom Lewis, would turn out as selfish and as ruthless as Barry Morrison in the end. Maybe even your sweet nature conceals an egocentric monster.

Never again, she reminded herself. Don't even think about it, Rose.

'No,' he said after a long pause, 'I guess it wouldn't, at that.' There was another silence, then Tom's cigarette arced through the air like a shooting star. 'I'd give a lot to meet the joker who hurt you, Rose,' he growled. 'Anyway, who knows? Maybe we'll see each other again some day.'

'Maybe,' she said, aware that he was deeply hurt. 'I'm sorry, Tom.'

'There's nothing to be sorry for,' he said with false brightness. 'It was only an idea. So—you'll go back to England, then?'

'I thought I'd spend a few days in Istanbul first,' she said, glad to change the subject. 'I really didn't see anything of the place before I came here.'

'Oh, it's a great place,' Tom enthused, his cheerful tone almost covering the hurt in his voice. 'You'll love it. Plenty to do and see there. I've had some good times in old Stamboul.' He pronounced it 'Stumble'. 'Come to think of it, Rose, I could show you round the sights if you liked. I know some great little——' He paused, then laughed quietly. 'No, I guess maybe not. Me getting carried away again. But you must let me give you some addresses.'

'I'd love that, Tom,' she said, aching for his hurt and disappointment.

A crunch of gravel heralded the approach of Selman Hristaki, carrying a lantern.

'Well, *mes enfants*,' he called cheerfully, 'aren't you coming in to dinner? Dorothy and Janine have made us a special farewell dinner.' He took each of them by an arm, and Rose blessed the Professor's kindly good sense. 'It is our duty,' he said gravely, 'to get thoroughly drunk tonight. After all, we may not see each other until the spring—eh?'

'Sure, Prof,' Tom agreed with a touch of dryness, 'let's go make whoopee!'

The goodbyes were surprisingly hard to make. Despite her aloofness and introspective mood, the others had all liked Rose; and it was odd how attached she had become to them all. Her oval face was wet with tears on the tiny station platform at Tuzluca, and she waved from her window until the little party of her colleagues was out of sight. Then she slumped back in her seat, Selman Hristaki's parting words still ringing in her ears.

'Goodbye, English Rose,' he had smiled, his dark eyes affectionate. 'And take my advice, child—whoever he is, wherever he is—forget him. He may have hurt you, but you still have it all to come. We all love only once in this life, and your time is yet to come. Believe me!'

Lulled by the rhythm of the tracks, she lay back, gazing out of the window with dim eyes. She didn't believe him. She couldn't.

Well, another episode in her young life was behind her. The little country train was carrying her steadily away from Agri; away from the rugged, savage hills, the cold, clean wind that blew across the Black Sea. Away from the strange man with the dangerous grey eyes who had knocked her sprawling with his rifle in a snow-filled cave. Who had he been? And where was he now? Crouching in hills somewhere, his rifle trained on another human being? Sitting, wolf-like and silent, in some Armenian tavern, his cold eyes continually flicking to the door?

'Well,' she muttered to herself, 'damn him, wherever he is!'

Nearly thirty-six hours later she arrived in Istanbul, and took one of the city's ancient taxis to her hotel, the Divan, an establishment which Tom Lewis had assured her was eminently respectable, in the central Taxim Square. A rainy October evening was settling over the huge city, and the many spires of its magnificent mosques were cloaked in purple-grey dusk.

Rose went straight up to her room, the clatter of the railway still dinning in her ears. The room was large, old-fashioned, and comfortable; and the wide bay window opened on to a vista of the square, the horns of the traffic rising musically upwards. Very few of the cars in the streets seemed to be under twenty years of age, many adorned with the immense wings and toothy grills that had been so popular in the 1950s; but here and there, the sleek passage of a Mercedes or

Jaguar hinted at the vast wealth that occasionally lay behind the poverty-stricken façade of Istanbul.

She gazed out over the shiny, busy streets, suddenly glad to be here, in this most romantic of capitals. Then, tired to the bone, she kicked off her boots and lay back on the creaking bed. It was, she had to admit, a deep relief to be away from the dig. It had been so cold . . . She was only now beginning to realise how very grey her moods had been at Igdir. Eastern Turkey was bleak and dark, and the work at the site had been unremittingly hard. Looking back, she could now see the reasons why she had chosen Igdir. The barren, rocky site had suited her inner mood of desolation. And maybe, if she was truly honest with herself, there had been more than just Barry on her mind. Maybe she had been experiencing some kind of inner crisis, a period of indecision as she waited for her life to take shape.

Ah well, the worst was probably over now. It was, at least, faintly exciting to be in Istanbul. She had gone through her obligatory period of sackcloth and ashes—that was what she had wanted, wasn't it?—and perhaps now things would look up. Her plans for the future were still vague. It was time to take a break, try and regain that holiday spirit.

Come on, Rose, she told herself, rubbing her eyes tiredly, start enjoying yourself, for God's sake. You're young, not exactly hideous, and more or less fancy-free.

Not very convincing, she realised wrily. Maybe if I said that every day for a month, it might make some difference . . .

Rose was slender and supple; it was only at her breasts and hips that her body became soft and full. The work in the trenches at Igdir had tautened all her muscles, flattening her stomach and straightening her back.

With her long, gleaming swathe of chestnut hair, her gentle, beautiful face, and her graceful movements, she attracted male glances wherever she went. Barry had told her that she looked like a Florentine Madonna of the fifteenth century. Her full mouth curled into a grimace of distaste as his memory crossed her mind, and she sat up abruptly, shaking the memory of his slow blue eyes out of her mind. Brushing her hair brusquely, she pulled on a pair of sandals, threw her astrakhan coat over her shoulders, and went out to find dinner.

The little restaurant at the back of the hotel was Westernised enough for the presence of a woman—a beautiful woman—eating alone not to attract hard glances. The waiters left her in peace as she ate a small, dull meal, a romantic thriller propped up on the tablecloth in front of her. She wasn't reading the words very carefully—the book was simply a means of indicating to any prospective Romeos that although she was alone, she was not in the mood for company. Not that she had ever had any trouble of that kind in Turkey, she reflected; they were surely the most polite and friendly people on the planet. She ate slowly and without interest, mentally planning her sightseeing expedition tomorrow. She would go to the fabulous Blue Mosque first—and then to Hagia Sophia. Strange to think that they were in Europe, those great buildings, while she was sitting here in Asia. Only a few miles away. Istanbul, indeed, spanned two continents, divided by the Bosphorous, and linked by the great Galata Bridge. She was now on the European side; once across the river, you were in Asia.

Where taps turned to the left, door-handles went up to open, light switches went down for off, and—well, anything could happen.

And strange that scarcely even the romance of her

setting could keep a flutter of excitement alive in her veins. Was she, at twenty-four, already an old maid, sapless and sour?

She paid for her meal, left a generous tip for having been left in peace, and walked back to her hotel.

She still felt tired and cold. Tired and cold right inside, next to the bone. The venerable boiler in the bathroom groaned and wailed with the effort of producing the quantities of hot water Rose demanded of it—but she was unmoved by its obvious misery. Three long months in the freezing mud and winds of Igdir had chilled her to the bone—and this was her first real bath (unless you counted the basinful of hot water that was all the archaeological site could provide) since she had left Istanbul for Igdir all those weeks ago.

She luxuriated in the warm water, feeling a pleasant sleepinesss wash over her. She had slept little on the train, she realised. And now that she was back in civilisation, she felt able to squander one of her treasures—a little scrap of heliotrope soap which she had kept wrapped in her flannel at Igdir, and whose delicate scent had allowed her to feel at least faintly feminine when up to the thighs in cold mud, looking for the three thousand and three fragments of a shattered Assyrian pot.

She slept like a child, deeply and dreamlessly.

The rain had gone by the next morning, and the fantastic horizon of the city, with its mosques and domes and minarets, was etched against a pale china-blue sky. The sunshine lifted Rose's spirits, and she left the hotel early in the morning, while it was still asleep. The whole city, indeed, was half asleep, and the bus that took her to the wonderful square where the Blue Mosque and Hagia Sophia stood side by side was half empty.

But her instincts gradually led her off the beaten

track of mosques and museums. Rose wanted to see the picturesque side of the old city, and she left the tourist route behind her by mid-morning, and wandered off down a side alley. Lunchtime found her eating pilaf rice and lamb in a tiny tavern crowded with workmen, and in the early afternoon she was strolling through the ancient district of Sehzadebasi. The streets were narrow, the houses dilapidated and almost incredibly ornate, and Rose found it all deeply charming. A tiny square with a tinkling fountain would give way to a salmon-pink palace, raising its peeling face out of the maze of shops and houses. Sometimes the streets were so narrow that barely two people abreast could walk up them. Sometimes they were so steep that Rose felt she needed a rope-ladder and pitons to negotiate the slippery cobblestones.

She had stopped on one of the broader streets to buy a bag of hot chestnuts when she noticed the car—a sleek Italian sports car, its gleaming grey matching oddly with the venerable street it was cruising down. She munched at the delicious, buttery chestnuts, watching the car with absent brown eyes. It stopped, eased itself into a parking place, and then the door opened.

Rose's heart jerked against her ribs.

The man who got out and casually locked the door was tall and wide across the shoulders. His dark suit was beautifully cut in silk; but she could never have forgotten that aquiline profile, nor the grey wolf's eyes that flicked up and down the street before he set off down the street opposite.

And if there were any doubt remaining, that walk dispelled it. No other man could move with the same poise, the swing of his body suggesting the muscular grace of some big leopard.

The Russian. Her mysterious assailant and rescuer. She stuffed the paper bag of chestnuts into her shoulder-bag with trembling fingers, her face pale. It was definitely her Russian. God! She stared around for a policeman. There was none in sight. And she discovered that without knowing it, she had shrunk back against the wall to escape those piercing grey eyes. But he hadn't seen her, that was certain.

She watched the tall figure disappear round the corner of the narrow street—and after a second's agonised hesitation, set off in pursuit. She would follow him to where he was going, then call the nearest policeman!

But fear was tugging at her heart as she ran after him. The roughness of that remembered blow served as a sharp warning that if he found her following him, she would receive no mercy.

She glanced up at the name of the street, struggling with her elementary Turkish.

The Street of the Fountain.

At least she wouldn't forget that name in a hurry.

As she rounded the corner, he came into view, and she stopped dead. He was buying a big bunch of lilies from an old woman on the pavement. She heard his deep voice as he made some joke, and caught another glimpse of that high-cheekboned face. What was he doing in Istanbul? The old woman was cackling as he set off again, the flowers cradled in the crook of one arm.

Rose scarcely had time to notice how picturesque the Street of the Fountain was. In the arches of a Roman aqueduct nestled a row of ancient shops, and Rose passed a coffin-maker's shop, a cat and dog hospital and a school of Islamic theology all side by side as she hurried after her quarry.

He moved fast and gracefully, and she had to trot to keep fifty yards behind him. And in a terrified way, she was beginning to enjoy herself immensely.

The shops gave way to a long wall of faded apricot

stucco, which bounded a large garden. A long row of towering palms leaned out over the street, and the luxuriance of the shrubs and trees in the garden obscured the house within. She could see only the slope of a tiled roof above the trees.

The man she was following pushed open the tall wrought-iron gate, and without looking back, walked into the garden.

Rose hovered on the pavement, her mind whirling. What to do? The faded number 37 beside the gate mocked her. Should she rush off to the nearest police station and—assuming she found someone who could speak English—denounce a tall, dark man at 37, Street of the Fountain? And what could she say? That he had knocked her over in a snow-filled cave high in the mountains, six hundred miles to the east?

'They'll tell me I'm crazy,' she muttered to herself.

She walked cautiously up to the gate, and peered through its ornate curls. The garden was ever so slightly wild. Through the shrubbery she could see a tantalising glimpse of a cream-coloured stucco wall. Somewhere, jasmine was still in flower, and the sweet scent drifted to Rose through the garden.

Slowly, carefully, she pushed the gate open and stepped through. Intense curiosity had got the better of her fear.

There was a paved path that led through the garden, and Rose followed it as silently as she could, clutching her shoulder-bag in both hands like a shield. The jasmine she could smell was a massive, flower-laden creeper that trailed from the slender pillars of a courtyard. This was obviously the back of the house; the courtyard led to an arched doorway, ornately decorated with Islamic tiles in faded blue and green. The wide swing door was ajar, and the mullioned windows above were empty. It was a beautiful, peaceful place. She poked her head cautiously round the door, and found herself looking down a corridor. A long Turkish carpet lay along the polished yew floor, and she could see what looked like a large drawing-room leading off a doorway not quite opposite where she stood.

Her heart in her mouth, she stepped inside and took one tentative step towards the door of the big room. She winced in near-pain as a floorboard creaked under her foot. There was a rustle in the room beyond, and a deep voice—a voice she knew very well—called out in faintly accented English, 'Is that you, Evliya?'

She froze in horror, wondering whether to keep silent or take immediate flight.

'Evliya?'

Quick male steps approached, then he was in the doorway. Her Russian. The grey eyes widened, and the long, strong fingers that were unfastening his tie lapsed into immobility. Then his brows came down grimly, and the saturnine mouth slanted into a forbidding line.

'Can I help you?' he asked, his fingers tugging at the lustrous silk of the tie. 'Are you looking for someone?'

'I——' Her throat was dry, her stomach uncomfortably hollow. 'I—I didn't mean to trespass,' she stammered. 'I just saw the garden—and—and smelt the jasmine.' Conscious of how idiotic she was sounding, she swallowed, and tried to muster her thoughts before that cool grey stare. 'I'm sorry to have intruded——'

'Not at all,' the man replied calmly. He was, she had to admit, extraordinarily handsome; and those bright grey eyes were made damnably striking by thick black lashes and large, attentive pupils. He drew the shimmering scarlet ribbon of his tie slowly from around his collar. 'Have we met somewhere?' he asked courteously, his eyes dropping to take in her figure.

'No,' she said quickly, praying he wouldn't recognise in her jeans and cotton jacket the rug-clad girl of the snow-cave. But, to her dismay, a dawning recognition was beginning to lift those level black eyebrows.

'By God,' he breathed slowly, 'the little archaeologist!' In a flash of unreasoning panic, Rose spun on her heel to flee; but with a leopard-like speed she was beginning to know and dread, he caught her arm, and spun her round with easy power.

'Let me go!' she gasped, desperately trying to break loose.

'I want to talk to you, you little fool,' he said, trying to hold her still. 'I've been looking for you over half of Turkey!'

'No!' She struck out at him in horror.

'I'm not going to hurt you,' he growled, warding off her clumsy blow. 'Take it easy!'

'Help!' Rose quavered, still struggling madly. 'Somebody, help!'

'For God's sake!' With terrified surprise, she realised that he was laughing under his breath, his eyes gleaming with amusement. She slammed her shoulder-bag against his hard chest, panting.

'Go away!'

'Will you please take it easy?' He grasped both her wrists in strong but not cruel hands, and forced her to stand still. Her chestnut hair tumbled around her face, she peered up at him with dread.

'Now listen,' he said gently and firmly, his eyes compelling hers to attend, 'I'm not going to harm a hair of your pretty head. Understand? I've been looking for you everywhere.'

She panted in silence.

'The last thing I want to do is hurt you. Do you believe me?' She stared, mesmerised, into the diamond depths of those fierce eyes, and somehow, the truth of what he was saying made her nod. Uncertainly.

'Good,' he purred. A slight smile tugged at the corners of his mouth. 'Now, I'm going to let your hands go. Do you promise not to take off like some startled doe?'

'Yes,' she whispered. She was beginning to feel that she had made a complete imbecile of herself. His hands relaxed their control of her wrists, and she took a hasty step backwards. The stunningly handsome face opposite her was impassive, but she was utterly certain that somewhere beneath that mask he was laughing at her.

'Now,' he said mildly, 'the door is open. Okay? But I'd be very glad of the opportunity to offer you a drink. And some dinner, perhaps. And above all, an apology.'

'An apology?' she quavered.

'Two apologies,' he corrected. 'Will you trust me?'

Suddenly, that high-cheekboned, incisive face was a mask of urbane good manners. There was not a trace, in this elegantly-suited and charming man, of the savage in the snow, whose wolf-bright eyes had burned into her very soul.

'Who are you?' she demanded, her courage returning in pace with her curiosity. 'You're no Russian.'

'Indeed, no,' he said. An expression of regret turned the corners of his eyes and mouth downwards. The mask would have fooled Rose utterly if she hadn't had the instinctive feeling that he was still deeply amused by her. 'I'm very much afraid I had to practise a minor deception on you and your elderly companion.'

'*A minor deception?*'

'Please.' The hand that reached for her elbow was kind but firm. 'Come into my study, *madame*, and let me explain everything. Is it too early for *raki*? I do not want to offend your English sensibilities any more than possible. But no doubt tea will be acceptable?'

Unwillingly, lulled by the quiet command in his voice, Rose allowed him to lead her into the room beyond.

CHAPTER THREE

THE room he led her into was a surprise. It was lined with books, the floor covered with rich Persian rugs. Even more to her astonishment, Rose recognised two fine ancient Assyrian vases on stands, and on the mahogany desk was a beautiful bronze head of a girl, most likely ancient Roman.

If this was the room of a bandit, then her captor must be an extremely successful bandit. And one with a most unbandit-like taste.

Dumbfounded, she sank into the chair he waved her to. He scooped up the telephone.

'Evliya? Tea in my study, please. For two.' He replaced the receiver, and leaned against his desk to study her better in the light. 'Have you recovered from your—er—little crisis?'

'I'm perfectly all right,' Rose said stiffly, trying to keep up an air of calm confidence despite her thudding heart. 'Who are you?'

'My name is Zoltan Stendhal.' His grey eyes watched her with the hint of a smile. 'Rather a difficult name, I agree. My mother was Hungarian, my father French, which explains the combination. It was fortunate, don't you agree, that there were no Russians in my ancestry?'

'And this house——' She ignored the smile. 'It's all yours? This study—everything?'

'Of course. Why not?'

'Why not indeed?' she retorted drily. 'Would you tell me, then, what would drag you away from all this luxury——' she waved around the room, '—to go roving around the hills of Agri dressed like a bandit?'

'That's a long story.' His smile was unchanging, but despite his relaxed stance, there was something in his poise that reminded Rose of a tiger in repose—ready to spring at a moment's notice. Underneath the expensive musk of his aftershave there seemed to lurk an aroma of danger which was continuing to make her feel distinctly uneasy. 'I'd better begin at the beginning,' he said gently. 'Like yourself, Miss Johnson, I am an archaeologist.'

'An *archaeologist*?' And then his use of her name sank in. 'How do you know my name?'

'I spoke to Selman Hristaki at Igdir,' he replied calmly. She blinked at him. 'He and I are old friends, Miss Johnson. In fact, he was rather amused to discover that your Russian officer was none other than my humble self.' He smiled at her expression. 'I'm very much afraid that the missile base was my own invention. As was my identity as a Soviet soldier. The reality was much more mundane—a simple matter of theft.'

'Theft?'

The door opened, and a young boy brought in a silver tray, then bowed himself out. Zoltan Stendhal poured tea into two cups, and settled down in the armchair opposite her. Rose stared into his face, all shyness gone. There was a hint of cruel power in his eyes which suddenly made her want to disbelieve the impression of civilised urbanity he had been so successfully projecting for the past few minutes.

'I don't believe you're an archaeologist at all,' she said, narrowing her eyes.

'Why not?' he asked mildly.

'You don't look like any archaeologist I've ever seen. You look like——' She hesitated, then decided not to pursue that point. 'And archaeologists don't roam around the hillsides carrying rifles and terrorising innocent people. I suppose you're going to tell me you were guarding some ancient treasure?'

'Something like that,' he smiled, ignoring her scorn. 'But what do archaeologists look like, my dear colleague? Is there a standard issue?'

She studied him. From the dark hair, silvered slightly at the temples, through that dazzlingly handsome face and poised body, down to his polished and no doubt handmade shoes, he was vibrant with an aura of male magnetism.

But he still didn't look like any archaeologists she had ever known.

'You look too prosperous, for one thing,' she said rudely. 'Archaeologists are generally about as rich as church-mice.'

'Here.' He tugged a big book out of one of the shelves, and passed it to her. The cover showed a striking photograph of two gigantic stone horses, and the title, in big white letters, read *The Babylonians*. The author was Zoltan Stendhal. There was even a photograph of his face on the back flap.

She flipped numbly through the pages.

'That's one of the reasons I look richer than the average archaeologist,' he said gently. 'I'm also a successful author. One or two of my books have even become standard texts in some universities. You may have read one.'

'*Pre-Sumerian Cultures*,' she said dully.

'That was one of my first books,' he nodded, and pulled a paperback volume off the shelf. She looked at the familiar blue cover.

'It was part of my second-year reading,' she said in a small voice. 'I never paid much attention to the author's name.'

'Now,' he smiled, 'is my credibility established?'

It had to be, she reflected wryly. The evidence staring her in the face was too powerful to be denied. Feeling more than a little embarrassed, she shrugged, dropping her eyes from his smile. 'Drink your tea,' he said gently, 'and let me try and explain what I was doing up in the hills that day. I'm technically what's known as a freelance archaeologist. But since I've made Turkey my home, I work very closely with the University of Istanbul. And that, in turn, involves me with the Department of Antiquities.'

Rose listened in silence, trying to work out her conflicting reactions to this extraordinary man, so full of surprises—some of them extremely unpleasant.

'In the past few months,' he went on, rising with taut grace and going to his desk, 'evidence has been trickling back to the archaeological world of an important discovery near Ispir. A lost citadel, no less. Precious and beautiful Sumerian artefacts began appearing on the black market—and I don't mean the usual bronze implements. I mean gold ornaments, precious stones. Things like this.' He passed her a ring. It was heavy, red gold, set with an eye of lapis lazuli and white enamel. Rose studied the softly gleaming thing, feeling that thrill of excitement that always came to her when she touched something beautiful from the remote past.

'It seemed highly likely that the Armenian hillmen—the real bandits of your imagination, Miss Johnson—had discovered a priceless cache somewhere up in the crags. And their good fortune meant a terrible loss for international archaeology. If they'd been left to plunder their hoard, perhaps causing irrevocable damage in the process, selling their finds to greedy collectors or unscrupulous private museums, the loss to human knowledge would have been tragic. Unique scholarly and scientific evidence might have been lost for ever.'

'I see.' She passed the ring back to him, beginning to feel that this was all a strange dream. Minutes ago she had been walking peacefully along an Istanbul street, not a thought in her head; and now she was sitting in a strange house, facing one of the most formidable (though admittedly extremely glamorous) men she had ever met, listening to a story that might have come from a television thriller.

'So you see,' he went on, 'that citadel had to be found. But Armenian bandits are dangerous.' He smiled without humour. 'Also ruthless and extremely cunning. So the Turkish government, in conjunction with other foreign governments who were interested, mounted a special operation to track down the source of the plunder—and I was invited to be the chief archaeological co-ordinator.'

'Why?' she asked.

'Because that area is familiar to me. Also, because unlike my more elderly colleagues, I am still young enough to scramble up and down hillsides in the snow and ice.' Rose glanced involuntarily at the breadth of his shoulders and the compactness of his hard-looking hips and thighs. 'Also,' he went on, watching her with bright eyes, 'because I know how to use a rifle, and because I do not mind being shot at. In the name of archaeology, of course.'

'Of course,' she said drily. 'And I suppose I shouldn't mind being deceived and battered black and blue—in the name of archaeology?' But despite her surliness, she had to respond to his laughter with a slight smile.

'Let's come to that by and by,' he grinned. 'On the morning that we met, Miss Johnson, I and my team were on the verge of finding what we were looking for. There were bandits in the hills, and we knew that they were planning to use the cover of the snowstorm to smuggle out a new consignment of treasures. Try and imagine the atmosphere—a group of tired, tense men, on the brink of both a great archaeological discovery and an imminent confrontation with dangerous thieves. We'd been living rough for a week, sleeping in the snow and living on iron rations. I'd been crawling along a line of crags, trying to stay out of sight, within a mile or two of the tribesmen—when suddenly I heard voices coming from a cave below me. I didn't realise at first that the voices were raised in song.'

A warm flush spread across Rose's cheeks.

'My guide and I were playing *kayiçi*. To try and keep warm.'

'An excellent idea,' he murmured. 'But will you believe me when I assure you that the very last thing I expected to find in those hills was a young woman playing *kayiçi* with an elderly man?'

'I suppose it seems very amusing to you,' she said shortly. 'You terrified the wits out of us both!'

'But I had no idea who or what you were.' He smiled disarmingly, showing perfect white teeth. 'You and your friend were wrapped in Afghan coats—I couldn't even see your faces properly. When you sprang up like that, my first thought was that you must be reaching for a gun or a knife. And in those parts, the rule is "shoot first and ask questions later".'

'But you didn't shoot,' said Rose, feeling an involuntary chill touch her spine.

'I wasn't completely sure that you were bandits. And when you collapsed in the snow after my little prod, all your beautiful hair tumbling loose, I knew at once that I'd made a mistake.'

'Little prod?' she echoed bitterly. 'I'm glad to hear that you're repentant, Dr Stendhal!' She stared at him hotly, remembering the pain and humiliation of that blow. Again, the inclination to disbelieve every word he was saying rose up strongly in her. And again, the reluctant truth forced its way upon her. It *had* to be true. And this extraordinary man had to be true as well.

'Miss Johnson,' he said, laying one broad hand on his heart, 'I am indeed repentant. If you knew how my unnecessary cruelty cut me to the heart, you wouldn't reproach me with those big brown eyes. But I had to temper my pity for you with the need to get you out of the danger zone as soon as possible. If you had been found by the bandits, or caught in the crossfire, you and your guide would have been riddled like colanders.'

'A poetic image,' she winced.

'The idea of masquerading as a Russian officer,' he said modestly, 'was a stroke of sheer genius. You see, although I could tell you weren't Armenian bandits, I still couldn't be sure of you. I had no way of telling you what was going on—it was, after all, a top security operation, whose existence was known only to a few dozen people, and we'd all been warned not to talk about it to anyone, no matter how innocent. My only option was to lead you back to safety as soon as possible.'

'Through a snowstorm,' she said bitterly.

'There was no other way.' She met the piercing grey eyes that smiled gravely at her, reflecting wryly that Zoltan Stendhal, with that face and built-in charm, would be able to talk the birds out of the trees. 'You were in serious danger. You might have been shot in an exchange of fire, or taken prisoner by the tribesmen. You could easily have frozen to death in your little cave—or starved. Or you could have fallen down a ravine in the storm. It may interest you to know,' he said silkily, 'that it's still snowing in the hills. But for my intervention, you would by now probably be just a rather shapely block of ice, Miss Johnson.'

'You're telling me I should go down on my knees and thank you?' she asked sarcastically.

'Well, I did save your life,' he smiled. 'And, incidentally, I jeopardised my own part in the operation, because I was away from my post for several hours, nursemaiding you and your guide.'

'Did you find your citadel?' she asked inconsequentially.

'Yes.' This time, there was unmistakable triumph in his face. 'A few miles beyond Ispir we found the source of the tribesmen's loot—a royal tomb of incomparable richness. Most of the treasure is gone, unfortunately—but where one such tomb exists, there will be others, and where there are several royal tombs, there will be a citadel nearby. A major excavation is due to begin early next summer, as soon as the snows have gone. This may, in fact, be the most important new find in Turkey since Pergamon.'

'Really?' Rose shook her head slowly, the tumblers of her mind slowly clicking into place. At last all the fragments of the story were falling into place, and despite her instinctive dislike of him, Zoltan Stendhal had impressed her. Why *did* she mistrust him? Simply because he was a handsome man, and she automatically distrusted handsome men? Or did her feelings go right back to her initial clash with him in the snows of Agri?

'You'll be reading all about it in the newspapers very shortly,' he said gently, as though sensing that she was still struggling to pinpoint her own reactions to what he had told her.

'I'll keep my eyes open,' she said drily. 'I've never associated archaeology with guns and bandits, Dr Stendhal. Do you often do this sort of thing for the police?'

'You're still sceptical,' he smiled. 'And the answer is no. I'm a peace-loving man, and I'm committed to my work. I'm committed enough to want to protect the world's archaeological heritage from people who would plunder it and destroy it.' He slid his hands into his pockets, and turned back to the window. 'Archaeology *is* associated with guns and bandits, my dear Miss Johnson. Like everything else that is precious and fascinating, it attracts thieves and conmen. But archaeology uncovers things that belong to all of us, from the greybeards and the scholars to the man in the street, the man who might look into a museum only once in his whole life. Our heritage is too important to be squandered or stolen. That you found me carrying a rifle in the name of archaeology, Miss Johnson, will suggest to you exactly how committed I am to my work.'

She glanced silently around the room. It was lined with books, some of whose titles she recognised. On every available surface there were fragments of the past—a blue faience vase from Egypt, some Sumatran bronzes, clay weights from Sicily, a slender Greek statuette on a plinth. Each piece telling of a dig somewhere, of hours spent in the sun or in the rain, hours of patient, dedicated work.

Yes, this man *was* committed to his work.

'I'm sorry if I seemed to doubt your word,' she said hesitantly. 'And I do agree with you about protecting Europe's archaeological heritage.'

'It's a struggle that never ends,' he nodded, turning those bright eyes back on her again. 'My little adventure up in the hills was a welcome change from routine, in fact. I've been struggling in the name of archaeology since I left university some twelve years ago, Miss Johnson. The struggle is always against human greed, human indifference. But greed doesn't necessarily show itself with a gun in its hand. More usually it comes with a request for planning permission and a fistful of dollars.' He ran his hand tiredly through his hair. 'I've been fighting the civil authorities for two years to try and stop the building of a supermarket on a prime archaeological site.' He tugged a slim book out of the shelves and showed it to her. It was called *Neo-Greek Settlements at Eminonu.* His expression was wry. 'There happens to be a priceless temple buried in that stretch of ground, one of the last traces of the cult of Artemis in the Near East. I've found some exquisite statuettes there. Now they want to build a five-storey hypermarket on top of it, and crush it all for ever.' He stopped, shrugging. 'I'm sorry—I must be boring you to death.'

'Not at all,' she said, fascinated. 'You're satisfying my curiosity, Dr Stendhal.' She looked up at him, noting the determination, the will-power, that lay in those level eyes. This would be a formidable adversary to have campaigning against you, that was certain! 'Are you based in Turkey permanently?' she asked.

'Only for part of the year. I'm an international gypsy,' he smiled. 'I tend to commute between various projects all over Europe. Archaeology can only be successfully carried out in the summer, as you know. I'm lucky enough to have a job that forces me to follow the sun. I'm a Fellow of various universities, and I do a little lecturing.' He gestured to the shelves. 'A little writing. But basically, I'm a practical archaeologist. I dig up the distant past, Miss Johnson.' He sat down opposite her, linking elegant, powerful golden fingers. 'And now, you must satisfy *my* curiosity. How on earth did you track me down to this house?'

'I was just sightseeing,' she confessed. 'I saw your car, and recognised you getting out of it. I ran after you, and——' she shrugged, 'here I am.'

'I see,' he purred, his eyes drifting over her figure in a frankly male appraisal. 'I'm very glad you dropped in, Miss Johnson. I had been wanting to apologise for some time. I called on Selman Hristaki before I left Igdir, but you had already departed. However,' he smiled, 'I was planning to come and see you tonight to explain things.'

'I don't believe you,' she scoffed. 'You don't even know where I'm staying!'

'The Divan, in Taxim Square,' he said calmly, and

quirked one corner of his mouth at her surprised expression. 'A very pleasant young Australian named Mr Lewis told me where you'd be staying.'

'Oh!' Rose blinked, taken aback. This was like some complicated game in which he had anticipated every move, won every round. As if sensing her residual puzzlement and frustration, Zoltan Stendhal shook his head.

'You are still angry with me, Miss Johnson. I realise that you're still confused. But it's really very simple. And I'm not the sadist you would like to think me. Please,' the curving smile held her spellbound, 'won't you let me make it up to you? And show you that I'm quite civilised after all?'

'What do you mean?' she asked.

'Dine with me tonight. We'll have a lot to talk about. After all, we have archaeology in common.'

'I'm afraid I won't be able to make it,' she said hesitantly.

'Why not?' He was so utterly sure of himself that her will faded.

'I—I've got a prior engagement——'

'You don't know a soul in Istanbul. Your friend Mr Lewis assured me that you'd be at a loose end, unprotected and unchaperoned.'

'I don't need protecting or chaperoning!'

'We shall see,' he said with sparkling eyes. 'Miss Johnson, I promised myself that when I next saw you, I would make it up to you. And I never break my promises. Now, I'll pick you up in my car at your hotel. Say six-thirty?'

'Dr Stendhal——' she began, trying to cling to her dignity.

'I think you must call me Zoltan,' he said in his deep voice. 'Dr Stendhal is terribly formal. And please don't argue any more, my dear Rose. I have a Hungarian temper that sometimes overrules my French gallantry.'

That was something she could believe!

'You seem to think you're irresistible!' she protested resentfully.

'I want to show you Istanbul, Rose. This is a city very dear to my heart. I know where to find its soul—the soul that has defied modernisation and twentieth-century squalor. The soul that still lives in Istanbul, beneath the veneer of Westernisation. And a quiet dinner *à deux* will provide the perfect framework for an evening of—shall we say, mutual exploration?'

The erotic undertone in his words brought the colour into Rose's cheeks. It was completely crazy, but she was as much under this man's spell and in his power as she had been that day in the hills. Her mind was spinning restlessly.

She was confused—and, she had to admit, more than a little panic-stricken. Zoltan Stendhal exerted a powerful magnetism over her, a feeling she hadn't known since Barry.

Yet it was a dangerous attraction, one that set her heart fluttering like a trapped bird against a windowpane. She wasn't used to the sort of sexy flirting that other people seemed to take so naturally. She wasn't used to *men*, in fact.

'You look like a startled fawn,' he smiled. She looked up with a troubled face, aware that he must find her terribly gauche.

'Dr Stendhal,' she said hesitantly, 'I don't know whether you're making a pass at me or not, but——'

'Making a pass?' He laughed happily as she flushed, showing excellent white teeth. 'I thought that phrase had gone out of use years ago!'

Furious with herself for her inexperience, Rose gritted her teeth. 'Whatever the phrase is,' she pursued doggedly, 'I just want you to know that I'm not available in that way.'

'No?' he smiled lazily.

'No,' she repeated. 'The fact is—I'm—I'm already engaged.' The clumsy lie spilled out before she had time to consider, and his alert grey eyes dropped to her left hand, ringless and slender.

'May I congratulate you?' he said with mocking irony. 'Yet your—engagement cannot be very passionate, my dear Rose.'

'Why do you say that?' she muttered, cursing the dull flush in her cheeks.

'Your fiancé hasn't been very prominent in your life. He didn't object, I take it, to your spending three months alone at Igdir? He didn't object to your coming to Turkey without him. He hasn't,' he finished gently, 'even bought you an engagement ring.'

Rose sat in miserable silence, aware of his inner laughter.

'You don't have to make up stories, Rose. If you don't want to come out with me, just say so. But don't make me feel that I frighten you. I don't—do I?'

Oh, but you do, she wanted to cry out! The sudden change in her 'Russian' was almost too confusing to deal with. Despite the beautiful study, despite the hefty book she had just been holding—despite his extraordinarily persuasive manner—she just couldn't reconcile the fierce wolf of the snowstorm with the urbane archaeologist who had now materialised in his place.

'You mistrust me?' he smiled, as though sensing her thoughts.

'It's a little difficult,' she confessed ruefully. 'Three weeks ago you were holding me up with a rifle. Now here you are telling me about Neo-Greek settlements at—where was it?'

'Eminonu.' He smiled again.

'Yes. I'm just wondering what's behind *this* mask.' She met his amused eyes defiantly. 'What new guise are you going to pop out in?'

'This is the real me,' he said solemnly. 'Zoltan Stendhal, archaeologist and part-time bandit. But let's discuss the whole thing tonight. Can't you think of it as just an ordinary evening with a fellow-archaeologist?'

With eyes like this, she reflected ruefully, no evening was going to be ordinary. She was utterly confused, and not for the first time on this strange Turkish holiday. That he attracted her profoundly was beyond doubt. Zoltan Stendhal provoked in her the sort of excitement, almost terror, that she had only read about. Not since Barry had any man affected her so intimately—and she had to admit that not even Barry had possessed this *presence*, this magnetism she was now experiencing.

The very strangeness of these feelings, though, was frightening. It had all happened so very suddenly! This plausible, beautiful stranger had simply bowled her off her feet——

'No,' she said decisively. 'I can't think of it as just an ordinary evening with a fellow-archaeologist.'

'Very well.' His eyes glinted. 'But can you resist the chance of seeing Istanbul as she really is?' He leaned forward persuasively. 'The places that I can show you aren't to be found in any guide-book, Rose. They're unique—part of the heritage of this city that foreigners never see.'

'I can live without that,' she said. But she was intrigued despite herself.

'Such a pity,' he said silkily, 'to come all the way to Istanbul, and to go away without ever having seen the soul of the city. Just think—you will never have seen Sarai Murat, the Jewel of the Bosphorus—or heard the tambur of Ali Akbar.'

'Who are they?' she asked.

'Come with me tonight, and you will see.'

Rose had the damnedest feeling that he was still

laughing at her. And then, she never knew why—perhaps out of pure pique, or because she suddenly wanted to take up the challenge in those diamond-bright eyes, she nodded briefly.

'All right, I'll come.'

'Excellent.' He seemed neither surprised at her volte-face nor triumphant. He rose fluidly. 'And now let me take you back to your hotel—you'll need some rest if you're going to enjoy yourself tonight.'

'Thank you,' she said ungraciously, sounding about as unenthusiastic as she felt. What on earth had possessed her to accept his offer? She was going to regret it bitterly, that was for sure? Hadn't she learned enough about attractive men to last her a lifetime?

'Tonight is in the wings of Destiny,' he smiled, catching her wry expression. 'You look like a person who worries a lot, Rose. Take my advice—and just relax for a change.'

But she had seldom felt so tense when, sitting in her bath in the late afternoon, she tried to analyse her whirling thoughts. Zoltan provoked reactions in her that were as paradoxical as the man himself. It had just begun to dawn on her that he was one of the most attractive men she had ever met. Perhaps *the* most attractive.

There was an aura of danger about him that both attracted and repelled her. Despite her air of defiance towards him, she was all too aware of the sway of his magnetism over her. It wasn't a reassuring feeling. Perhaps it was asking too much of her instincts to simply accept the transformation of villain into hero, just like that. Perhaps there was something else, too—a recognition that Zoltan affected her in a way that other men had never done, not even Barry. He frightened her—and yet there was a maturity about him that made her want to respect him. Perhaps it was his very maturity that was affecting her so profoundly.

Because with Zoltan, she knew unmistakably that she was dealing with a man. A mature man, with a man's powerful mind that a man's body; a man who would make no concessions to her youth and inexperience. She didn't fool herself where sex was concerned; if Zoltan could get her into bed, she knew that he would. And then——

She soaped her flushing cheeks. What was wrong with her? It wasn't usual for her to feel like this, to speculate about a stranger's sexual manners.

Perhaps she had been in Turkey too long. The Middle-Eastern decadence was getting to her.

But who could tell what the night would bring? She trusted Zoltan, at least, to show her a side of the city which she would never have come across. He had made it, after all, his home, and he seemed to know it well. But after that . . .?

She peered at her watch, lying on the chair. Damn! There was very little time left. She was going to have to postpone all worries and analysis for a while, and do what he had advised her, simply let things happen . . .

Someone watching Rose Johnson clamber out of her bath, clutching a large towel, would have seen a remarkably pretty sight. A luxurious shampoo had restored the sheen to her dark chestnut hair, and it tumbled in a curly swathe down her supple back, as glossy as any racehorse. Rose didn't have the dramatic looks that often pass for beauty with film stars or models. But the sweetness of her features and the gentle grace of her movements were deeply feminine. There was an inner beauty about her, a kind of soft, almost luminous radiance, that set her apart from other women—and always would do, when those beautiful bones continued to make her beautiful even in old age. And that soft, wide mouth invited a man's kiss the way a rose asks to be inhaled or a fine wine asks to be tasted.

She hadn't come to Turkey expecting to spend much time in the high spots, and she had only one decent dress in her suitcases. It was a Chinese silk dress that Freddie had brought her the last time he had visited England. The delicate material was light enough to have inveigled its way into her packing, although she had scarcely expected to wear it. The material had been soaked in water, then exquisitely folded and crushed into millions of flower-like petals. Tied into shape, it had been left to dry—so that when opened, it was covered with a garden of patterned creases and folds.

That also made the material cling to her body rather more than she liked, and she surveyed herself dubiously in the mirror. The silk whispered dangerously close to her skin at hips and breasts, showing a tantalising glimpse of the soft curves beneath as she moved.

Damn! She was going to be awkward enough as it was, without having to worry about whether or not she was giving Zoltan Stendhal the wrong message tonight. Improvising hastily, she knotted a silk scarf at her neck, hoping somewhat in vain that the floating ends would protect her modesty.

There were butterflies in her stomach as she pulled on stockings, and sat at her dressing-table to brush her hair back. Yes, she realised without vanity, those months of hard work at Igdir had done her good. She looked beautiful, and almost simple in a 1930-ish sort of way.

Make-up? Her skin, finer than the hand-woven silk she wore, was too good to need foundation, but she brushed mascara lightly on to her lashes to make them sootier, and smoothed her full lips with a gloss that she hoped was suitably cool and chaste in colour.

Months at Igdir had left her skin pale, and her tan had faded almost to nothing. Reluctantly, she dusted the bare minimum of blusher on to her perfectly-moulded cheekbones. She didn't want Zoltan to think she was anaemic.

Rose was still hovering over sandals or court shoes when the bedside telephone burred.

'A gentleman to see you, *mademoiselle*,' said the receptionist.

'Yes,' said Rose nervously. 'Tell him I'm coming down now.'

He was waiting for her in the foyer, a tall figure as handsome as Lucifer in evening dress. The austere cut of the suit set off his taut, powerful figure to perfection, making him sexy, dazzling. With the thoughtless grace of a fencer, he came forward to take her fingers. The warmth of lips against them seemed to send a tingling heat up her cool arm and straight into her beating heart.

'You look like a princess,' he smiled, drawing her close to his side as he escorted her out, past a goggle-eyed receptionist. Through the suit, she was tremblingly aware of fluid power against her body, the hardness of muscle that had been honed to a dizzying potency.

'Where are you taking me?' she asked, trying to keep her voice cool.

'To the Garden House of Suleiman the Red,' he informed her, as casually as if he had said 'the Dorchester'.

'That sounds like something out of John Buchan,' she smiled.

'You'll like it,' he promised, glancing down at her from his dark height. She caught the musky sweetness of some aftershave. And underneath it, nerve-stretchingly, that familiar smell of masculine power, intoxicating and frightening.

The Maserati was waiting, an elegant shape against

the busy Istanbul street. Rose let him usher her into the leather seat, and drew a deep breath as the engine purred into life. His very proximity was making her heart pound, as though there were some fierce drug—on his velvety skin perhaps, or in those diamond-bright eyes—that seeped from him into her system.

My God, she thought weakly, now I know what they mean when they say a man gets under your skin!

She lay back in her seat as the car surged forward with sleek power.

'You're the only archaeologist I know who can afford an Italian sports car,' she ventured. He smiled.

'I'm not bound to any salary. And my books bring in a fair amount. As for this——' he patted the leather-clad steering wheel affectionately, 'I bought her with the proceeds of a minor speculation on the stock exchange.'

'Not all that minor, by the looks of it,' she commented. 'You know shares well?'

'They're one of my hobbies,' he acknowledged. 'I use what I make on the stock exchange to buy the little luxuries in my life.'

'Such as?' she couldn't resist asking.

'Oh—a holiday home here and there. A cottage in Jamaica where I spend six weeks of the year. Some of the antiquities you saw in my study. And evenings like this one.' He glanced at her, and smiled at her expression. 'I'm not exactly poor. Does that make me a crook?'

'Of course not,' she said hastily, and he turned his attention back to the road. The aquiline profile was lean and hard, and Rose found herself wondering how many women before her had sat in this passenger seat staring at that fascinating profile. She studied the silver streaks over his ears and the few sharp lines at the corners of his mouth and eyes, and decided that he must be under forty—maybe as young as thirty-five or six. Very young to have come so far in an exacting profession, and to have a string of respected books behind him, though with that superb body and those virile good looks, it was hard to guess his age precisely.

'Studying me?' he asked, shifting gear smoothly into a bend.

'What does Zoltan mean?' she asked by way of a reply.

'It's the Hungarian for Sultan,' he told her. 'My mother was rather a romantic.'

'Oh, it suits you,' she assured him, smiling to herself. 'The only other Sultan I knew was a Bengal tiger.'

'I know the gentleman,' he smiled. 'But he is in the circus. *This* tiger is on the loose.'

'Tell me,' she said, trying to sound relaxed and poised, 'is your life always as exciting as it's been over the past few weeks?'

'I enjoy excitement,' he shrugged. 'Most men do. But I don't necessarily seek it out.' He glanced at her quickly. 'You've made up your mind that I'm a decadent playboy, have you?'

'Not exactly,' she said guiltily. 'From what I've seen of you, you work too hard to be decadent. And I really enjoyed your book at university.'

'Don't tell me you actually remember your university textbooks,' he mocked.

'It wasn't all that long ago,' she said defensively. 'Besides, it was a good book. I learned a lot from it.'

'Indeed?' His smile was almost wry. 'You make me feel dreadfully old. I suppose I seem ancient to you?'

'You can't have been very old when you wrote *Pre-Sumerian Cultures*,' she replied, thinking that far from ancient, he was probably at the most attractive age a man can be.

'I was twenty-six,' he acknowledged. 'Just over ten years ago.'

'You're thirty-seven now, then,' she murmured, and he nodded.

'Yes. And you?'

'Twenty-four,' she replied, thinking how absurdly young it sounded.

'What sign are you?' he asked casually.

'Virgo.'

'How appropriate,' he grinned. 'I'm Scorpio.'

You would be, she thought tartly, but didn't articulate the thought. Scorpio—the ultra-masculine sign, redolent of sex and dark mystery. It suited him.

They had driven out of the city, and were now on a tree-lined avenue. In the darkness ahead, a string of fairy-lights was now visible.

'The Garden House of Suleiman the Red,' he murmured.

CHAPTER FOUR

THE night sky was blue velvet, sprinkled with diamonds. A silver sickle of a moon glittered on the tumbling waters of a fountain in the centre of the courtyard where jasmine trailed, and the heady scent of late summer roses hung on the air. The Garden House was already quite crowded, the patrons at the candlelit tables happy and elegant in their finery; but the waiter bowed deferentially to Zoltan and led them to a quiet alcove under a pergola of roses, overlooking the courtyard.

'How lovely!' Rose couldn't help exclaiming, enchanted by the place.

'This is a little bit of old Istanbul,' Zoltan smiled, the candles glowing in his smoky grey eyes. She leaned forward to stare over the fountain at the domed roof beyond, from where a sinuous Eastern melody was being softly plucked on a zither, and Zoltan studied her.

'You are beautiful, my Rose,' he murmured. 'This place suits you. Despite your English looks, there is something almost Oriental in you. A hint of amber, perhaps. Or a taste of myrrh. Are you sure there was no Persian beauty in your ancestry?'

'Quite sure,' she said, disturbed by his compliments.

'Ah, that English *sangfroid*,' he mocked, 'how delicious it would be to ruffle it, to see the doe darting off through the woods!'

'So you could give chase?' she retorted. 'No, thank you, Mr Tiger. I'm not going to arouse your interest that far!'

He grinned. 'Now you *have* intrigued me. Do you know men so well?'

'Well enough,' she rejoined coolly.

'Let's come to that later. Now, tell me about your parents, Rose. If your mother isn't a Persian beauty, then what is she?'

'My parents are both dead,' she said dully. Even now, the pain of saying that made her lashes droop over her brown eyes.

'I'm sorry,' he said, all trace of his bantering gone in a second. 'I wouldn't have joked if I'd known.'

'A car accident, when I was fifteen.' She gave a tiny, painful shrug. 'My brother looked after me.'

'There must be more to it than that,' Zoltan said gently. He reached out, brushing her lustrous hair back, and lifted her chin so he could look into her eyes. 'It still hurts you, doesn't it? Tell me about it.'

'There's little to tell.' She stared into the candle-flame. 'We were a very happy family. My brother Freddie was in his final year of medical school then. He's eight years older than me. Mum and Dad were driving down to London from where we lived in the Midlands. Two lorries collided on the ice, and their car was between them. According to the doctors, they can't have known very much about it.' She drew a deep breath. 'Freddie came rushing to school to tell me, at eleven-thirty in the morning. They took me out of the Maths class to meet him.'

Rose fell silent, her hands curled empty in her lap.

'You don't have to say any more,' Zoltan said softly. 'I know what it is to lose one's parents. But tell me what happened after that. How did you survive?'

'Freddie got an internship at the local hospital,' she told him slowly, thinking back to those grim years. 'We moved to a flat to be together—we didn't want to be separated—and just struggled on.'

'Are you very close to your brother?'

'We weren't before our parents died, but we grew

very close afterwards. I guess the difference between our ages had always come between us until then.' She smiled at him. 'You can't really be interested in all this.'

'Where is your brother now?'

'He's a surgeon at a big hospital in Chicago,' she told him. 'He's much in demand.'

'And you miss him?' The grey eyes were damnably intelligent.

'Now and then.' His gaze was beginning to disconcert her, and she sat back, away from the candle-glow.

'How rude I am,' he said urbanely, 'you must be starving. Would you like me to order the starter?'

'Yes, please,' she nodded.

'Then I choose oysters and champagne,' he smiled. One lift of an eyebrow brought the waiter hastening over, and Rose watched him as he ordered in fluent Turkish. He could not know it, but he had drawn more from her in a few minutes than most men did in months. There was something about that compelling gaze that seemed to make her transparent, as though her soul were crystal and he were able to see into its very depths.

'What about you?' she said as the waiter whisked off. 'My little life must seem very dull to you, Dr Stendhal.'

'I still haven't heard you say my name,' he said in his soft, deep voice. He took her fingers between his, and turned her palm up to study it. 'Suddenly, my dear Rose, I have an urgent desire to hear you say my name. It is Zoltan. Say it.'

'Zoltan,' she whispered, the name like a spell on her lips. A shiver passed through her, as though she was afraid that the simple act of saying his name might bind her to him in some potent charm.

'Very good,' he smiled. He drew one finger

lingeringly down her palm. 'Why does your hand tremble so?'

'I'm cold,' she snapped, snatching her hand away.

'Yet the night is warm.'

'I find it cold,' she said stiffly. What on earth had got into her? Zoltan was being so warm, and she was reacting so stupidly. She had expected that he was going to try and charm her tonight—why was she shaking like this? Perhaps because she had severely underestimated the effect that Zoltan's charm would have on her!

To her relief, the waiter materialised with a platter of baby oysters on the half-shell and a bottle of vintage Bollinger. She watched as the golden wine foamed in the crystal as he poured, trying to summon back her poise. It wouldn't do to let Zoltan see that she was in any way disturbed by the spell that he was so expert at casting.

'I hope you like oysters,' he said, deftly lifting one from its bed of mother-of-pearl. He laid it on a slice of brown bread and butter, squeezed lemon over it, and passed it to her. The morsel was delicious, and she said so.

'Do you treat all your ladies like this?' she asked, licking the tart juice from her fingers.

'Only the ones I think will appreciate it.' His face was mocking, and she couldn't help smiling in return. She had certainly never met anyone quite like Zoltan Stendhal, and it wasn't always easy to define her own reactions to him. He said things, for example, that would have been insulting on anyone's lips but his, and got away with it every time.

'To all bandits,' she said drily, toasting him with her glass. The wine was fragrant and clean, tasting of a distant summer.

'To all bandits,' he agreed. 'Without whom you and I wouldn't be sitting here tonight.'

'I suppose you're going to be asked to direct the excavation at this new site you've found?' she enquired.

He shook his head.

'Unfortunately not. Next year is going to be very busy for me—I'm going to be lecturing at Cambridge in the spring, and in the summer I'm directing an excavation in southern Spain.'

'It sounds as though you're much in demand.'

'I keep busy,' he shrugged. 'The new excavation at Igdir will go to the University of Istanbul. I was just co-ordinator of the search team. This,' he smiled, 'happens to be my holiday period. Winter is the off-season for archaeology in Europe, as I'm sure you know. I could have taken up an invitation to excavate in New Mexico, where some interesting Aztec remains are turning up—but I decided to take a break.'

'What will you do?' she asked, studying the calm, assured face and capable hands. 'Won't you get bored?'

'I hope not.' His eyes were bright. 'I'm in the middle of another book at the moment, and that should keep me out of further mischief for a month of two.'

'What's it about?'

'A new field for me—the Etruscans.' He looked up at her, and she smiled.

'The most mysterious people in ancient history.'

'Exactly. There's so little known about them, and so little of their civilisation left, that the whole concept of research seems pointless.' His eyes were thoughtful. 'Yet I think I've got a few new things to say. They were in many ways the most fascinating people who ever lived. They pre-dated the Romans, of course. And their religion seems to have been dark and eerie, and peopled with monsters.' He smiled gravely. 'They may have practised human sacrifices, and worse.'

Rose shuddered slightly. 'The Etruscans aren't exactly my favourite topic,' she acknowledged. 'But they've always fascinated me. I'd love to read what you've written about them.'

'Would you?' He met her eyes and nodded. 'I'll show you one or two chapters some time. Now tell me, Rose—what drew you to archaeology? It isn't exactly a subject to lure a beautiful young woman.'

'Oh, it is! I love it. I always have done, ever since I worked on a dig during a school holiday when I was sixteen.' She smiled, her mind going back to that sun-drenched holiday in Ireland and the first stirrings of fascination with the past which had awoken in her during that busy summer. 'It was a very humble affair—just a dig round the foundations of an old castle. We didn't turn up anything very exciting. But from that summer, I knew what I wanted to be. As soon as I left school, I did archaeology at college, and——' The fleeting memory of Barry made her shy away from that part of her life, and she shrugged quickly. 'Well, here I am.'

Zoltan was watching her carefully, his eyes damnably intelligent.

'I should say that you're a good archaeologist,' he judged. 'You have that love for the subject. It shines out of your eyes.'

'I'm not bad,' she said uncomfortably. 'I need a lot of experience.'

'And Igdir was your first professional engagement?'

'Yes.'

'Strange that you should have chosen to bury your talents in such a remote and lonely dig,' he suggested, wiping his fingers with a wedge of lemon.

'Selman Hristaki happens to be a brilliant man,' she said stiffly.

'Of course. But completely crazy about Assyrian sites that have very little interest for anyone else. What made you choose Igdir?'

'It sounded very interesting,' she said, unable to keep a defensive note out of her voice.

'And you needed the solitude?'

'Partly,' she admitted unwillingly.

'An unhappy love affair?' She looked up angrily, resenting the way he was probing a painful area of her life.

'That's my business.'

'I see,' he nodded, as though she had answered his question.

'I just wanted some time to think,' she said, wishing he'd direct that piercing gaze somewhere else. 'That's all. Okay? Now, can we talk about something else, please?'

'As you wish.' He smiled. 'I now have a better idea why you're so afraid of men, though.'

'I am *not* afraid of men,' she retorted.

'No?' His eyes glinted.

'No,' she repeated, beginning to feel very uncomfortable. 'I can take them or leave them.'

'A very practical attitude,' he remarked, and his obvious amusement made her flush.

'I'm certainly not one of those women who're unable to do without a man,' she said sharply. She was aware of sounding absurdly prim and immature, but she just couldn't help it. He put her on edge the whole time, made her feel that she had to be on the defensive. She was beginning to wish—despite her attraction towards him—that she hadn't come tonight.

'So you're impervious to Cupid's darts?'

'I didn't say that,' she muttered. 'I just don't think I need romantic entanglements of any kind.' Goaded by his smile, she went on, 'All right, so I did have an unhappy experience, and I don't want to talk about it, that's all.'

'Sure,' he shrugged. 'If the wounds are still tender——'

'I just don't like having to talk about my private life with strangers, Dr Stendhal.' Rose tried to fight down her shaky anger. Damn the man! He got through to her so easily . . . 'I'm beginning to wonder why you asked me out in the first place,' she said shortly.

'Does a man need a reason to ask a beautiful woman out?' His smoky smile mocked her. 'You intrigue me, my sweet Rose. It's not every day one finds an English virgin crouching in a cave, high on a savage Turkish mountainside.' She looked up at him sharply at the word 'virgin'.

'You're determined to make fun of me, I see,' she said coldly.

He poured champagne into her glass with a slow smile.

'Ah, Rose,' he purred, 'perhaps we'd better keep off personal topics for a while. Okay?' He took one of the scarlet lilies out of the bowl on their table, snapped off the long stem, and leaned forward to slide the brilliant flower into her silk dress. The thrilling grey eyes looked into hers as he adjusted the delicate petals.

'A truce?'

His fingers had no more than brushed her skin through the silk, yet it was as if the contact had trailed fire over her. She was conscious of a crawling pleasure that radiated across her skin from his touch, warming her. A truce? She smiled inwardly. No. Because in that minor, sensual act of gallantry, Zoltan Stendhal had declared war on her, as surely as ever a man declared war on a woman he desired.

'A truce, then,' she nodded, knowing that, at that instant, Zoltan had begun laying siege against the citadel of her passions. And in his mind's eye, she knew, this softly-smiling man could already see the flames!

'Now,' he murmured, leaning back as the waiters

cleared the table, 'tell me what your plans are for the winter. Have you got another dig lined up?'

'Not yet,' she confessed. 'I thought I'd do some sightseeing in Turkey for a few days, and then head back to London. I've got a little flat there—and I'll probably be able to get my old part-time job back at the University.'

'Tutoring?'

'Yes,' she nodded. 'Some first-year tutoring, and cataloguing work in the archives.'

'Hmmm. Dull work for such a lovely Rose, surely?'

'What makes you think I'm not dull?' she retorted.

'Dull? A dull woman would never have chosen to come to Turkey to work, Rose. A dull woman would never have followed a dangerous Russian spy to his house.'

She had to smile at her suspicions. Yet there *was* a Slavic hint in Zoltan's magnificent face; it lay in the way those stunning eyes were slightly upward-tilted at the corners, giving him something of the expression of a tiger or a leopard. And the darkness of his crisp hair, highlighted with threads of silver over the temples, added drama to a face that was already superbly virile.

'Well,' she shrugged, 'I have my career to think of.' She broke off, as the rose-coloured lights in the courtyard faded. A rustle of anticipation swept through the crowd as the velvety Turkish darkness settled over the candlelit garden house.

A group of musicians had arrived, wild-looking men in the turbans and flowing robes of some hill tribe, and were settling themselves next to the fountain.

'What is it?' Rose asked Zoltan in a whisper.

'The floor-show,' he smiled. 'I told you this place was a little bit of old Istanbul. Watch now.' He sat back a little, so that he could observe both the courtyard and Rose's face. She stared at the musicians with interest. They certainly didn't look like the commercialised artistes of the tourist circuit; their hawklike faces were intent, dark.

And a breathless hush crept over the Garden House of Suleiman the Red.

Into the silence crept a whispering hum, the savage whine of some primitive stringed instrument played with a bow. The sound was electrifying in the stillness, with the crescent moon gleaming down.

And now other sounds fell into place, the serpentine melody of a pipe, weaving itself like a cobra through the rhythm of a drum whose insistent beat, pitched to that of the human heart, grew deeper and stronger.

Rose glanced at Zoltan uneasily. This was a wild music that tugged at the heart and stirred the pulses, a music that grew out of the rugged hills and the darkness of the human heart, before time began or man was civilised. His eyes cautioned her to watch and be silent. She turned back, aware that the pulse of the music was faster now. And that the throbbing rhythm was taking her heartbeat with it.

An even more savage strain was creeping into the music. The musicians were stooped over their instruments, urging the melody to an almost unbearable pitch of tension and excitement. Rose's nerves were on edge, her breathing quicker in response to her altered heartbeat. And then the music abruptly stopped, leaving a quivering silence.

From somewhere, an intense spotlight began to glow. It illuminated the figure of a woman lying prone in the centre of the courtyard. She seemed almost naked. A deep sigh went through the audience, almost too low to be heard. Then, with agonising slowness, the music began to seep back into the silence, note by note, weaving gradually into a pattern of sound more complex and thrilling than anything Rose had ever known. Again she looked at Zoltan, almost in fear. He reached out his hand, and without hesitation she took it, comforted by the strength in the fingers that closed around hers.

And the figure on the floor began to move. With incredible control and grace, she seemed to rise out of the earth, like an adder rearing itself, her gleaming torso swaying in time to the throb of the music. This was the very breath of the East, an art and culture that was too profound for Western intelligences, a promise of such giddy sensuality that it actually frightened the senses.

At last she was upright. Her face was sensuous and cat-like, full lips curving into a slight smile, her long-lashed eyes almost closed in a kind of ecstasy. With delayed shock, Rose realised that but for a silk veil that drifted between her thighs from a gold chain around her supple waist, and a covering of gold leaf at the tips of her breasts, the dancer was naked. Her body, the colour of liquid bronze, made not the slightest concession to Western taste. She was full, intensely feminine, the power of that pulsing stomach and those long legs matched by a fullness at breasts and hips that Rose knew would excite any man of the East.

She was aware of Zoltan's thumb caressing the back of her hand, teasing the sensitive skin. Her own fingers trembled in his, like the wings of a trapped butterfly.

And the dancer slid into a slow, almost shockingly erotic dance, gliding around the edge of the floor. There seemed hardly to be a bone in her body. She was all pulsing muscle, her movements smooth and supple. And every motion, every glance from those coal-black eyes, sent a promise thrilling out to the watchers. A promise of giddy, intoxicating delight.

As the music spun faster and wilder, her movements became more abandoned. Her eyes were shut tight now, her hips thrusting and revolving in a pattern of desire, her arms reaching up to embrace an invisible guest to whom it seemed her very soul was open.

Dimly, Rose was aware of a trickle of sweat down her spine. She could scarcely tear her eyes away from the dancer; her fingers were knotted in Zoltan's with aching tension.

Now the dancer was down on her heels, her thighs apart as she swayed slowly backwards. Her spine arched with incredible suppleness as she threw her head back, lifting her arms to encircle the lover that the music was providing. Her hips lifted, swaying, the taut muscles of her stomach and abdomen contracting and pulsing in an unmistakable, delicious surrender.

Somewhere in her mind, Rose was horrified, shocked into astonishment. Yet somewhere else, her own heart was pulsing in time to the dancer's, her own soul yearning for that surrender, that intoxication. She wanted—she couldn't tell what she wanted. Zoltan's eyes were burning into her, yet she was terrified to turn and meet them. She clung to his hand, as though a sea of passion were tearing at her, threatening to sweep away all her inhibitions, her moral decisions, her notions about the world and about the people in it.

The music was lashing at her senses now, its savage rhythms impelling the dancer on the floor to new peaks of ecstasy, her body writhing and thrusting as though possessed by some terrible masculine devil who was discovering every secret of her soul and heart, whose desire was pushing her beyond human limits.

Shuddering, Rose tore her eyes away. It was too much to watch, too erotic, too unashamed!

Zoltan's eyes were deep on hers, his calm smile as intimate as a kiss.

'Don't you like it?' he murmured, his deep voice caressing her.

'She's—she's shameless!' Rose protested huskily.

'What has she to be ashamed of?' he asked. His long, strong fingers laced themselves slowly through hers, locking his strength into her weakness. Somehow, the contact touched her on the raw, like the most erotic of caresses, and she shuddered again, her eyes closing involuntarily. The primitive, exotic music was making her giddy.

'Is she not beautiful?' Zoltan purred. 'Like you, my sweet musk-rose. You have no more reason to feel shame or fear than she does.'

'Stop,' she whispered, 'don't talk like that——'

'Watch her,' he commanded. 'And see the soul of a woman of the East, Rose.'

She dragged her heavy eyelids open. The music had reached a plateau now, whirling around the courtyard like the desert wind that had given it birth a million years ago. The dancer was moving among the tables now, her arms held high, her body glistening with sweat.

The glow of the candlelight caught the faces of the guests who stared at her as she passed by, lighting the dark gleam in a man's eyes, the half-smile that curved mysteriously over a woman's mouth. There seemed to be no envy among the Turkish wives and partners who sat with their men; rather, an excitement, a veiled passion. As the dancer passed by an elderly couple, Rose watched the old woman's eyes glitter as she smiled at the dancer.

And then she knew what it was. That although she was old, her body no longer supple and strong, the old woman had been touched to the soul by the dance. Because the dancer had portrayed her inner soul, the inner woman that could never grow old or die inside her.

In fascination, Rose watched the dancer approach their table. The coal-black eyes were gleaming under the thick lashes, the smile on the sensual mouth wide and inviting. She paused for a second beside Zoltan, smiling down at him, her hips and waist swaying in slow, voluptuous invitation. With a sense of shock, Rose caught the smell of her, a musky perfume that was spicily underlaid with the woman-smell of her body.

Then she was in front of Rose herself, the dark eyes holding hers. What did that smile mean? The solidarity of some secret sisterhood? The professional smile of a dancer to a patron?

She passed on, the light gleaming arabesques off her pulsing body; and then, with a breathtaking suddenness, she was gone. The music was silenced, and nothing was left of the spell but the tang of musk in the air, and the quivering silence of a near-hypnotised audience.

The lights glowed up again, and the audience burst into rapturous applause, shouting and clapping. The courtyard was suddenly restored to its innocent calmness again, the fountain tinkling merrily as though mocking the ease with which they had fallen under that potent charm.

As though released from shackles, Rose sagged back in her chair, still clinging to Zoltan's hand. He leaned forward in concern.

'Rose?' His fingers touched her cheek. 'Are you not feeling well?'

'I'm fine,' she said weakly. 'I—I just felt a little faint——' What was happening to her? A strangely dreamlike feeling was settling over the evening, as though events were running out of her control. She had never, in all her young life, had experiences like these, been with a man like this. She just wasn't ready. Even the most sophisticated woman might have been bowled over by the combination of Zoltan's magnetism and the seductive location. But for Rose, the impact was that of a totally alien culture, of people and places that were beyond her experience. He made her feel as though she had tasted a wine that was far, far stronger than she had anticipated, and had drunk too much . . .

'Perhaps I shouldn't have brought you here,' he wondered to himself, watching her. 'Here—drink some more champagne.'

The sparkling wine revived her. Embarrassed at her ridiculous weakness, she sat up straighter. A buzz of conversation had risen up again, and everyone was turning to their dinners with relish. A waiter had brought a sizzling tray of *shish-kebabs* to their table, and was now ladling a fragrant mountain of pilaf rice on to their plates.

Predictably, Rose found she had little appetite for the exquisite-smelling food.

'You enjoyed Sarai's dance?' Zoltan asked casually.

'Not very much,' she said primly. 'It was a little too graphic for my taste.'

'Oh?' He helped her to a skewer laden with charcoal-roasted chunks of lamb, red peppers, mushrooms and golden marrow. 'I take it you disapproved, then?'

'I just didn't like it,' she said, conscious of sounding horribly English and old-maidish. The delicious smell tempted her. 'How am I meant to eat this?'

'With your fingers and with your teeth,' he told her, picking up a skewer and tearing the meat off it with white teeth. She followed suit gingerly. The hot meat was delicious. With a little exclamation, she leaned forward to wipe a dribble of juice off her chin. Turkish customs were proving a trifle embarrassing tonight!

'What didn't you like about Sarai's dance?' he enquired, his handsome face impassive.

'I don't think any woman should make herself into a—a—sex object for men to leer at,' she rejoined. One dark eyebrow quirked.

'Is that what you think Sarai was doing?'

'There was a certain art in her—performance,' Rose admitted grudgingly. 'But in this day and age, women should have more self-respect than to dance like—like——'

'As if some man was making love to them,' he finished calmly. A touch of colour came to her cheeks, and she bit into a succulent mushroom without replying. 'Yes,' he nodded slowly, 'the dance is unmistakably sexual.'

'It's disgusting,' she flared up suddenly. 'Why, it was just an imitation of——' She broke off again.

'Of?' he enquired silkily.

'Of something that should be private,' she choked.

'You mean of lovemaking,' Zoltan smiled, those dazzling eyes bright with amusement.

'Yes.'

'Is not all dancing exactly that, my dear Rose? A poetic evocation of the act of love?'

'But that woman was just throwing herself at some man's feet,' Rose protested. 'A woman ought never to be so available, so—so—subject to any man's desires. She's his equal, isn't she?'

'Everywhere except in the bedroom,' he smiled, his voice deep and sensual. 'In the bedroom, a man must be unquestionably the master.'

The colour in her cheeks now deepened into a blush.

'What you say degrades a woman's role in society,' she snapped.

'Oh, nonsense,' he smiled. 'You talk like the virgin you are. A man's love does not degrade a woman! It elevates her, makes her something special in the universe, unique and adored. What Sarai expresses in her dance is not abasement or degradation, my dear Rose—but the joy, the exultation of a woman who knows in her heart that she is desired, loved by her man.'

'But she surrenders utterly to him,' she retorted, looking away from those piercing eyes.

'Of course. A sweet surrender, sweeter than anything else between the womb and the grave in this short life of ours. The relationship between a man and a woman is the highest achievement, the most profound and important thing in human destiny.'

'Really?' She tried to disguise the trembling that his words had sparked off in her, and toyed with her champagne glass in apparent casualness. 'I think there are more important things, Dr Stendhal.'

'Such as?' he prompted, his passionate mouth curving into a smile that brought shadows to the golden skin of his lean cheeks.

'Such as a career. A vocation. Art, music, painting.'

'What is a career compared to love?' he scoffed. 'The greatest men and women throughout history have thrown everything they had to the winds for love. Art? Do you not know that all art is as surely the expression of love as Sarai's dance was tonight? No art can be produced without love. The greater the lover, the greater the art.'

'A very clever little proverb,' she sneered, dabbing juice off her lips. 'Love is just a word, Zoltan. A word invented by a man to trap a woman into giving him the things he wants.'

'What things?' he enquired softly.

'Her body to satisfy his desires,' she retorted. 'Her adoration to flatter his ego. Her service for his comfort. And in the end,' she concluded, her brown eyes dark under veiled lashes, 'her suffering to amuse his cruelty.'

'*Ma chérie*,' he said softly, 'someone has hurt you very badly. Very badly indeed.' Rose looked away from the compassion in those diamond-bright eyes.

'I've learned my lesson well,' she said coolly. 'And I'll never be hurt again.'

'Then you refuse to consider another man?' he asked, his smile taunting her. 'Will you die an old maid, Rose of England?'

'I am indifferent to such things,' she replied coldly.

'Will you ever take on another lover?'

'Perhaps on my own terms,' she said. His bark of laughter startled her. 'What's so funny?'

'My dear Rose! And what are your terms?'

She attacked her *shish kebab* to hide her confusion.

'That's my own concern,' she muttered.

Zoltan leaned back in his chair, rocking with laughter. As handsome as Lucifer in evening dress.

'Your company is delightful,' he spluttered, his sparkling eyes set in laughter-lines that made them all the more stunningly attractive. 'Don't ever ask me to let you go, Rose. Your dialogue is irresistible. Now—please, what are your terms?'

'Freedom,' she snapped, angered by his amusement. 'I want to be free to do what I want, go where I please. I'll never be tied down by another man. I'll never give everything up again. I'm going to be my own woman!'

'Ah,' he sighed, his laughter still tugging at that fascinating mouth, 'and they wonder why so many Western marriages end in divorce! Here in Turkey, they have a different approach.'

'That's because they're still living in the distant past,' she rapped out. 'Women in the West want more freedom, Zoltan. They're not going to be tied down any more!'

'No? Your talk is full of freedom and independence, Rose. Are those qualities really so important?'

'They're better than servitude and bondage,' she rejoined.

'And yet,' he said in his velvety voice, 'it seems to me that love calls for exactly those things that you renounce—self-sacrifice, devotion, a willingness to give up one's selfishness, to meet another person halfway. How can love survive if neither of the partners will give an inch? That is the way to sterility, despair, failure.'

She sat silent.

'Perhaps,' he smiled, 'when you have crossed the Rubicon you will feel differently about all these things.'

'What do you mean—when I've crossed the Rubicon?' she asked sharply. But he was looking up with a smile.

'Here is someone who knows more than either you or I,' he said, rising, and Rose turned to see a dark woman in a black evening dress arrive at their table. Her shiny black hair was tied in an elegant chignon, and there was a smile on her cat-like face.

'Rose, I want you to meet Sarai Murat. Sarai, this is Rose Johnson, a friend from England.'

Rose's heart skipped a beat as she recognised the sooty-lashed eyes and exotic smile of the dancer who had been holding the whole place spellbound a few minutes ago. She gave Rose's hand a firm squeeze, then kissed Zoltan on the cheek.

'It is good to see you, *mon cher* Zoltan,' she said, her voice unexpectedly low and smooth. 'And good to see you, *mademoiselle*.'

'Pleased to meet you,' Rose said awkwardly.

'Won't you join us for coffee and brandy, Sarai?' Zoltan invited, oblivious of Rose's angry glance.

'Thank you,' the Turkish woman smiled, allowing Zoltan to ease her into a chair. The warm, dark eyes met Rose's. 'Did you enjoy the show?'

'Very much,' said Rose, the stiffness of her tone suggesting exactly the opposite. But Sarai seemed not to notice.

'I'm glad,' she said simply. 'The musicians were good tonight.'

'Yes,' Zoltan agreed. 'I have been telling Rose that this is one of the few places in Istanbul where the belly-dancing is authentic. And certainly the place with the most beautiful dancer.'

'It is always hard to remember that you are a Frank,' Sarai smiled. 'You talk just like a Turk sometimes, Zoltan. He is impossible, *n'est-ce-pas*, Mademoiselle Johnson?'

'Impossible,' Rose agreed drily. Sarai's face, she noticed, was clear-eyed, relaxed. Almost the face of a woman who had been made love to. I wonder, Rose thought suddenly ... and blushed to find her thoughts asking questions she had never dreamed of considering!

'My mother was a dancer,' Sarai explained, accepting the brandy glass the waiter deferentially offered, 'and her mother was a dancer before her. As with many skills in Turkey, it is passed on in my family from one generation to the next.' She smiled at Rose, her feline face irresistible. 'And you, *mademoiselle*—what is your skill?'

'I'm an archaeologist,' Rose volunteered. 'A very junior one.'

'Ah, then you and Zoltan will have much in common,' she nodded. 'Not so?'

'Yes,' said Rose noncommittally, sipping the fiery brandy from the balloon glass. She was aware of the admiring male glances that Sarai was attracting from the tables around, and she wondered fleetingly what sort of contrast her own pale-skinned, slender looks would make against this voluptuous, copper-skinned beauty.

'Rose is a liberated Western woman, Sarai,' Zoltan smiled. 'She has been telling me that she wishes to be free, never to be imprisoned by any man.'

'Of course,' Sarai nodded, her heart-shaped face solemn. 'Only a mad person wants to be in love, *n'est-ce pas*?' She rolled her dark eyes expressively. 'The heartaches, the passions, the jealousies, the storms and the tempests—Allah, love is for stronger spirits than I!'

'Truly?'

'I swear it,' Sarai nodded earnestly. 'After every man.' The glitter in those dark eyes brought a chuckle from Zoltan.

'You are incorrigible, Sarai! How is that Persian dancer you were so mad about last week?'

'Ah, the faithless wretch,' she glowered, 'he ran off with another dancer.'

'Another Persian?'

'As you say, *mon cher*. And worse, another man. Never trust a Persian dancer,' Sarai said to Rose, turning her dark, mock-melancholy eyes on her through Zoltan's laughter. 'A pity—he had the body of a gazelle, the face of Adonis.'

Rose gulped brandy in silence.

'You cannot mean to tell me that you are at present unchaperoned?' Zoltan enquired, his grey eyes smoky with amusement.

'Of course not,' the dancer replied, raising her slender brows over her brandy. 'Didn't I tell you?'

'Let me guess,' Zoltan volunteered. 'A Greek? A Frankish millionaire?'

'Darling, a Count,' Sarai whispered in a thrilling voice. 'No less. A Belgian Count!'

'I didn't know the Belgians had Counts,' Rose said innocently.

'Of course,' Sarai assured her. 'And so rich! He is not so young as he was,' she sighed, 'and not so athletic as the Persian——'

'Sarai,' Zoltan smiled, 'you're going to outrage Rose.'

'—well, let us say that he has a mature charm all of his own,' the dancer concluded. As if by accident, she looped one finger in the string of pearls around her neck, drawing attention to the rich, expensive-looking jewels. But the humour in the dark, liquid eyes that glanced from Rose to Zoltan was hard to resist, and they both burst into laughter as Sarai preened herself.

'By God, a fine necklace,' Zoltan judged, leaning forward to study it. 'You must have captivated him, my dear.'

'He is secure in my nets,' Sarai grinned, showing small, pearly teeth. 'Speak of the devil—I must fly, my friends.'

Rose glanced across the courtyard to see a portly, middle-aged man in an expensive-looking cape hesitating under the colonnades. The knob of his stick was pressed to his moustache, his eyes fixed adoringly on the dancer.

With fluid grace, she rose, gathering her stole around her.

'I hope I shall see you again, Mademoiselle Johnson,' Sarai smiled. 'And be careful of this half-Hungarian devil next to you!' She stooped, and kissed Zoltan tenderly on the cheek. 'Goodbye, my handsome nursemaid,' she said to him, almost too low for Rose to hear. Then, with a bright wave, she was gone. Rose watched her join the Belgian Count, who received her with adoring arms and an expression of utter devotion. When Zoltan sat down again, his eyes were laughing.

'I sometimes think that Sarai has discovered the secret of perpetual youth,' he said, shaking his head.

'Why did she call you her nursemaid?' Rose asked inquisitively.

'Her little joke,' he shrugged. 'I once looked after her when she was ill. Now, what about some *halva* and figs?'

'Tell me about Sarai,' said Rose, unwilling to let the topic rest. This glimpse of Zoltan Stendhal as Florence Nightingale was intriguing her. 'When did you look after her, and why?'

'Ah,' he said, tapping her neat little nose gently, 'the

sharp female nose. You think Sarai is an old flame of mine, I suppose?'

'She's very attractive,' Rose said obliquely. 'What was wrong with her?'

'Well,' said Zoltan, obviously reluctant to discuss the topic, 'Sarai hasn't had a very happy life, Rose. She's been unlucky, despite her talent and looks. Three years ago she had a bad nervous breakdown. She was drinking heavily, not really in control of herself at all. Some man was at the bottom of it.' He caught her glance, and smiled. 'Not me, I hasten to add. She was in a bad way, poor Sarai, ready to end it all. She came to stay at my house for a while.'

'You took her in?'

'She needed help,' he said calmly, 'and she wasn't getting it. I gave her a room in my house, put her to bed, and generally pampered her. Tender loving care, so to speak.'

'Hmmm,' Rose said speculatively. Women would be queueing up to have nervous breakdowns if shown the prospect of being pampered in bed by Zoltan Stendhal afterwards! But she was touched, too—touched and somehow impressed.

'It's not easy nursing someone through a nervous breakdown,' she said thoughtfully. 'My brother's a doctor, and he's told me that several times. I can see now why she looks at you like that.'

'How does she look at me?' he asked, raising one eyebrow.

'As though you were her guardian angel. She obviously adores you.' Rose toyed with her wine-glass, looking at the bubbles in the golden liquid. 'Did you—did you have an affair with her?'

'That's a very personal question, Miss Johnson,' he said drily. But there was a glint in his eyes. 'No, I didn't have an affair with Sarai. She was sick, and she needed help. I didn't take her into my care for the purposes of seducing her.'

'Not even afterwards?' she asked boldly. 'After all, she's a very sexy woman. And you——' She stopped herself. 'Weren't you tempted?'

'Temptation and sin are quite different things,' he said, amused. 'You're no theologian, Rose. I first met Sarai at this place, many years ago. We became good friends—and that in itself would have been enough to prevent us from having an affair. It would be silly to jeopardise a good friendship by letting sex take too large a part.'

'Yet you acknowledge that at least some sex was there?' she prompted.

'You're as sharp as a Persian lawyer,' he said. 'There is always a certain amount of sexual attraction in any friendship between a man and a woman. It's inevitable. But it's up to each one to decide whether to allow attraction to become desire. And then to allow desire to become passion.' He drained his glass. 'If you could have seen poor Sarai as she was then, you wouldn't be asking these questions, Rose. She was half her normal weight, shaking and crying. You could almost see the clouds of depression over her. She was on the brink of total collapse.'

'And you brought her back?' Rose asked softly. 'That was quite an achievement.'

'It was worth it,' he said, watching her with warm grey eyes. 'It's worth it every time I see her dance and hear her laugh. On the other hand, she broke most of my crockery, and terrorised my faithful servants into resigning.' He grinned. 'Some more brandy?'

'I've had more than enough, thanks,' Rose decided. She was becoming aware of the potent spell that this man was weaving around her. His formidable sex appeal was hypnotic; but this revelation of his kindness, even tenderness, towards a sick woman opened up new areas. Dangerous areas.

It was one thing to acknowledge that he was stunningly attractive. It was quite another to find that he was eminently lovable. And to let attraction, as he had said, become first desire, and then passion!

Get out now, Rose, said a quiet little voice inside her. Go home, go to sleep, and forget all about him. Or else your heart will end up in more pieces than Barry Morrison ever broke it into!

'It's getting rather late,' she said reluctantly. 'I think I'd better get back to my hotel . . .'

'Late? The moon is still high, and the sun is hours away yet.' The candlelight glittered in his amused, beautiful grey eyes. 'If you're ready to go, then let's go, by all means.'

'But not home?' she guessed in a small voice.

'Home? Of course not. The night is yet in bud!' Zoltan smiled, sexy quirks appearing at the corners of his mouth. 'We have a duty to bring it into full flower.'

CHAPTER FIVE

THE quayside was dark and silent as Rose scrambled on board the yacht, Zoltan's fingers locked round her wrists.

'But—but where are we going?' she was still complaining. 'Is this boat yours?'

'Of course,' he answered, stooping to unhitch the mooring line. Bewildered, she watched his lithe figure. He had driven her down to the banks of the Bosphorus from the Garden House of Suleiman the Red, refusing with maddening secrecy to say where he was taking her.

She hadn't been able to believe that he meant to go sailing at this hour of night—it was half an hour to midnight—and had merely gaped as he led her to the large motor-yacht moored underneath the Galata Bridge.

Now, though, as the current of the river slowly but steadily tugged the boat into mid-river, her heart lurched.

'Where are you taking me?' she demanded for the tenth time.

'For a swim,' he said, and she caught the gleam of his smile in the velvety darkness. He let himself into the wheel-house, and turned on the engine.

'*A swim?*' she goggled, following him into the cabin. The motor was throbbing under her feet, and the big yacht had begun to glide steadily upstream. 'A swim where?'

'The Bosphorus is a trifle dirty,' he told her, his face bathed in green light from the instrument panel he was checking. 'So we're going up to the Black Sea. Near Irva.'

'I don't believe you,' Rose blinked.

'It's only ten miles or so. We'll be there in half an hour.'

'But——' She shook her head slowly. 'You're outrageous, Zoltan! You can't just kidnap me like this! I don't want to go to Irva—and certainly not at midnight. Take me back!'

'Why reject the idea before you've even seen the place?' he smiled. 'Who knows, you might even start enjoying yourself.'

'I want to go back!' She could hear the rising note of panic in her own voice, and was unable to control it.

'You're intolerable,' she went on shakily. 'You really believe all that rubbish about a man being the master——'

'Only in the bedroom, I said,' he interrupted coolly. 'You can spit like a cat anywhere else—but in the bedroom a man must unquestionably be the master.' He surveyed her tense expression calmly. 'Do you truly want to go back to Istanbul?'

'I just want to be consulted now and then,' she said bitterly, feeling that he had once again made her seem immature and unsophisticated. 'I'm not a slave, to be led around the place.'

'I thought you might enjoy the surprise.'

'Being with you is one long surprise,' she retorted. It was true; like a deceptive current, the force of his personality was continually cutting the ground from under her, sweeping her off her feet. 'You remind me of the sea in Cornwall,' she went on, trying a wry little smile. 'We used to swim there when I was a child. You'd be paddling away quite happily, and suddenly you'd look up at the shore and find that you'd been washed a hundred yards up the coast by the current, far beyond the safe area.'

'I promise not to let you drown,' Zoltan smiled. 'I'm not as ruthless as the sea.'

'But you're just as deceptive.'

'Well,' he shrugged, 'make your mind up.'

Rose sat in silence, clasping her hands nervously. If she said yes now, she would be truly throwing all her doubts and fears to the winds. In the space of a few short hours, Zoltan had made an indelible impression on her. From being a feared stranger, he had swiftly become something more. Perhaps he was even on the brink of becoming a lover. She felt a slow shiver creep down her spine.

The dreamlike feeling was wearing off abruptly. This was for real—real people, real emotions. Did she want to go any further? *Yes*, her heart was whispering, *yes, you do! You want this more than anything in the world.* Like you wanted Barry? she asked herself bitterly. Do you actually need to be hurt, Rose? When are you ever going to grow up? As though he had guessed her thoughts in some eerie way, Zoltan left the wheel to come over to her.

'Are you thinking about your ex-fiancé?' he asked quietly. 'Tell me something, Rose. Do you still love him?'

'Of course not,' she snapped, his words touching her on the raw.

'No? Then why can't you stop thinking about him? The truth is that you like hugging your misery to your chest, don't you?'

'That's a despicable thing to say,' she rejoined, wincing.

'But true. You're so in love with self-pity that you can't think of anything else. All you want to do is to be left in peace to cling to your dismal little memories.'

'I've made up my mind,' she snapped. 'I do want to go home. Now. Please!'

'*Petite idiote*,' he said gently, caressing her cheek with the back of his hand. 'You look so disarmingly pretty when you get angry. But you aren't really angry with me, are you? You're angry with yourself because your little tragedy is over.'

'What do you mean?' she glowered, twisting her face away from his caress.

'I mean that it doesn't hurt anymore. What that man did to you. You can't even whip up a good weep about him any more, can you? All your much-vaunted wounds have healed over long ago.'

Rose sat in stunned silence, staring out over the moonlit water as his words sank in.

And slowly, a small smile tugged at her lips.

'You may have a point, at that,' she said softly. 'But that doesn't mean I'm coming with you on this midnight jaunt.'

'Yes, it does,' he whispered, stooping to kiss her softly on the forehead. His lips left a rose of flame on her skin as he walked back to the wheel.

She did not protest as he gunned the engine, sending the yacht surging up the dark river. He was right—as always. Her crying over Barry had ended long ago. The sensation, deep in her heart, was a mixture of laughter and tears and wonder. She tried to fight the tears—or the laughter, she wasn't sure which—down. But a little sound escaped her lips. Zoltan didn't turn around, but she sensed that he was smiling to himself.

'Feeling better?' he asked quietly.

'Yes,' she nodded, absurdly, weepily happy.

'Good. And now, let's get to know each other, Rose. Properly. Agreed?'

'I've changed my mind again,' she replied obliquely. 'I've decided I'm coming, after all.'

'Even though you're convinced I'm a tiger?' he grinned.

'I shall be on my guard,' she replied primly. 'I shall be on my guard.'

True to his words, the white yacht was gliding out

of the northern channel of the Bosphorus by just after midnight, and the Black Sea was opening up in front of them.

In the silver moonlight, it lived up to its name, as dark as wine, its wavelets lapping at the hull of the boat.

'Isn't it beautiful?' Zoltan called from the wheel, and despite her forebodings, Rose had to agree. The peace of the scene was deeply beautiful. On the shoreline, no lights glimmered, but the moonlight was bright enough to reveal the palms and thickets of spruce behind the silver-white beaches.

'How far is your cottage?' she enquired.

'Not more than a mile from here. We don't go as far as Irva. You'll see it, just beyond the next cape.'

He led her on to the deck, and from the rail at the prow they watched the sea ahead. The dark bluff of a headland gave way now to a small cove, sheltered by two arms of land that stretched out into the sea. A white crescent of beach glimmered in the moonlight, and as the yacht entered the little bay, a few minutes later, Rose could see that there was a cottage of some sort set back from the beach. A grove of palm-trees towered over it, and there was a pathway that seemed to lead to stone stairs from the beach up to the little garden in front of it.

'I come here a lot in the autumn,' Zoltan told her, switching off the engine. 'This is my retreat.'

'It's beautiful,' she said with truth as the boat glided silently through the calm sea into the cove. The stars in the velvety sky above glittered on the water, and all about was solitude and peace.

About a hundred yards from the shore, Zoltan threw out two sea-anchors and a drogue to stop the yacht from drifting in the tide. The rustle and murmur of the sea was deeply soothing, and they could just hear the breeze among the palm-trees on the land.

'Got over your temper yet?' he enquired with a smile.

'More or less,' Rose said grudgingly. 'But I still think you're the most high-handed man I've ever met.'

'I shall take that as a compliment,' he purred. 'Now, shall we wash off the last of your indignation with a swim?'

'Yes,' she agreed—and then stopped short. 'Have you got a woman's bathing costume on board?'

'I'm afraid the *Argo* isn't a haberdasher's shop,' he said drily. 'What need have you of a bathing costume? We're alone, and it's night.'

'You're here,' she pointed out acidly, 'and there's a very bright moon above.'

'Yours won't be the first female body I've seen, Rose,' he said gently. 'I don't think you'll be different enough to shock me.'

'That's not the point,' she snapped. Ready to curse with vexation, she looked from the broad-shouldered man opposite her to the tempting glint of the sea. 'I'll swim in my underwear,' she decided.

'Oh, Rose,' he sighed, 'you're a very repressed young woman.'

'What do you mean, "repressed"?' she demanded angrily.

'You didn't approve of Sarai's dance. You spent most of the dinner wiping every drop of juice off your pretty chin. You didn't want to come for a swim. And now,' he concluded, leaning back and folding his arms, 'you're too ashamed of your body to swim in the sea as Nature intended. When are you going to stop being afraid of life?'

'Who says I'm afraid of life?' she rejoined, her face hot as she realised what a prude he must think her.

'You are,' he insisted gently. 'But you can't stay terrified of every drop and splash that life throws your way. You hoist your skirts up like an insane old maid at every glint of reality.'

'Oh, really?' she enquired sarcastically. 'That's why I spent the last three months up to my waist in mud at Igdir, I suppose?'

'Besides,' he said, changing the subject deftly, 'If you wet your underclothes, you'll merely have to take them off afterwards to let them dry. Now, would you rather be as naked as a dolphin *in* the water, or as naked as a dolphin *out* of the water?'

With an exclamation of annoyance, Rose turned away. Shrugging, Zoltan pulled off his evening jacket, and hung it on the coach-roof.

Rose gritted her teeth, staring out to sea. She hated the implication that she was a prude, afraid of life. Afraid of men. If only Zoltan knew how attractive she found him! She was holding back not because she wanted to, but because she desperately needed to defend herself. She was too innocent, too open to carry through the kind of flirtation that Zoltan or Sarai Murat would enjoy.

She felt trapped, frightened, vulnerable. And she didn't know what to do about it.

As though he guessed something of her inner turmoil, Zoltan padded up behind her, and rested his hands on her shoulders, drawing her gently back. With an inner trembling, Rose felt the warm velvet of his naked chest against her back.

'Do you really hate my company so much?' he asked softly.

'You know I don't,' she replied, her voice low and shaking. 'But you're right—I *am* afraid.'

His lips brushed the back of her neck, his warm breath raising the fine hairs on her arms and down her spine.

'Why?'

'Being with you is like—it's like walking a tightrope.

I don't know how long it's going to last, or where I'm going. The only thing I do know is that sooner or later I'm going to slip and fall.'

'Rose.' He turned her gently to face him. He was wearing only his black trousers, his wide shoulders and chest naked in the moonlight. 'Listen to me. Life is not for the faint-hearted.' His fingers bit into her shoulders, his diamond-grey eyes burning into hers. 'If you just cower away from it, it will pass you by—or else trample over you. You have to embrace it, accept it. And the same applies to love. Your sterile little dreams of finding a relationship in which you can be free, give nothing and take nothing—that's all cotton-wool, Rose.'

'I don't——' she began shakily, but he cut through her sentence.

'Listen! Any man who would permit you to have that kind of relationship with him would be no man at all. He would be a man without manhood, a lover incapable of satisfying you.'

'Stop!' she gasped, his words setting her blood racing in her veins. 'I don't want to hear any more!'

'You do,' he said fiercely. 'Life has mountains of achievement, my dear Rose, and it has valleys of mediocrity. If you are ever to experience the shuddering delight that love can bring, the blossoming of the soul, the fire that burns and does not consume, then you must be prepared to embrace life, to climb its mountains. And only when you yourself are capable of giving all to a man will you know true love, true ecstasy.'

Her breath was harsh in her dry throat, and but for his strong hands on her shoulders she might have fallen.

'Zoltan,' she whispered, drowning in the power of his eyes, 'don't talk to me like this! Let me go!'

'One last word. You imagine yourself an ice maiden, my dear Rose. Better that you should accept that you are flesh and blood. Or one fine summer's day the sun will touch you.' His lips met hers, hard and quick. 'And you will melt.'

Leaving her swaying, he unbuckled his belt, and started to take his last garments off.

Hypnotised, she could only stare at him. The muscles on his smooth torso pulsed under the velvety skin. He was superb, his waist and hips supple as a dancer's, his shoulders rugged with mature male power. Across the breadth of his pectoral muscles, thick dark curls spread in a wide triangle. Savage power, lithe beauty, a dazzling grace, all were there. His legs, long and knitted with powerful muscles, were those of an athlete. Hot and dizzy, Rose managed to tear her eyes away as he slid the black briefs off. Knowing that he was naked, only feet away from her, was sending her blood-pressure surging upwards.

'Join me,' he said, and she could hear the smile in his voice. Then there was came the sound of a big body cleaving the water, and when she looked again, he was gone.

His head broke the surface of the dark water, fifteen feet from the boat, and she saw him strike out in a smooth crawl away from her.

Her mind made up, she slipped into the coach-house and slid her sandals off. The rustling silk dropped around her ankles, and then she was naked.

The cool night breeze on her bare skin was intoxicating, innocently sensual. With a scrap of ribbon, she pulled her long dark hair into a ponytail—and then, naked as the day she was born, clambered cautiously down the taffrail into the sea.

It was colder than she had anticipated. An autumn cool had drifted down from Russia, and she gasped as she slid into the dark waves, her skin contracting at the cold contact. She pushed away from the yacht in a stately breast-stroke. The water was deliciously cold inside her thighs and over her breasts, and once the initial shock was over, the sensation was exquisite.

As Zoltan had predicted, the last of her ill-temper vanished in the beautiful water. She rolled on to her back, throwing out her arms and legs, feeling the sinews stretch. Lovely! All that hard work at Igdir had honed her body down to a springy suppleness she really enjoyed. She felt fit, young.

It was wild and beautiful here. The Islamic crescent of the moon hung high in the inky heavens above, the stars sprinkling the sky from horizon to horizon. The great column of the Milky Way, heaven's dazzling backbone, lit the dancing waves around her. White on the water, like a great albatross, the yacht swayed at anchor.

'Zoltan!' Her voice drifted across the water. She looked around for him, then caught the white foam around his shoulders as he swam up to her.

'Glad you came?' he enquired.

'Very,' she laughed. His hair was sleeked back, emphasising the masculine lines of his face. Without thinking, she drifted up to him, smiling.

'You are lovely in the moonlight,' he said, reaching out cool fingers to caress her wet cheek. And then, as though the deep, invisible current had pulled them together, Rose found that she was in his arms, the tips of her breasts brushing against the rough hair on his chest, his thigh sliding warmly between her legs.

'Rose, sweet Rose,' he whispered, his hands sliding across her shoulders, drawing her to him. 'How well that name suits you.' She closed her eyes as his mouth brushed the soft skin next to her eyes. 'You are as innocent, as fragrant, as lovely as the flower you're named after,' he said. Dizzily, she was aware of his body close to hers, its warmth tantalising in the cool, dark water.

'You're very gallant,' she answered, trying to force a

laugh to her tight throat. But the moonlight in those smoky grey eyes was going to her head like wine.

'You make it almost compulsory for a man to be gallant,' Zoltan smiled, letting the current drift her away from him.

With pain, and yet relief, she felt his arms release her, and she floated on the swell with pounding heart.

'Do you bring all your women here to be seduced?' she asked unsteadily.

'You asked the same question at the Garden House,' he smiled. 'You seem to think I have a kind of circuit in mind for you, well trodden by the feet of your predecessors.'

'You mean you haven't?' she asked, throwing back her head to gaze up into the moon.

'You think like a truly devious woman sometimes,' he said, amused. 'Despite the ice-water in your veins, you and Sarai are sisters under the skin.'

'I doubt it,' she rejoined. The moonlight gleamed on the sleek muscles of his back as he swam away from her. She paddled after him. He seemed as at home in the water as on the land, his body sliding through the water like some big, compact fish.

'Have there been many?' she enquired, floating on her back beside him. 'Predecessors, I mean.'

'I'm not a gelding, Rose,' he replied silkily. There was an ironic quirk to that passionate mouth. 'I like women.'

'And women like you,' she prompted.

'Well, do you like me?' he enquired, one eyebrow raising at the temerity of her implied question. She trod water in an awkward silence for a few seconds.

'Like you in what way?' she asked uneasily.

'In the way you've been talking about,' he said with a quiet chuckle. 'As a prospective seducer.'

'Of course not,' she retorted, suddenly feeling all her naked skin go cold.

'No?' One stroke of those powerful arms brought him suddenly face to face with her in the sea. 'It seems to me you're in deep water, Rose. In more ways than one.'

'How—how deep *is* it here?' she choked, now anxious to change the subject.

His magnificent face, fierce and beautiful as a tiger's, smiled at her.

'Ten miles down—ten feet. Why do you ask? You will not sink as long as I am here. Now tell me, my sweet musk-rose, why are you so interested in the numbers of my conquests?'

'I thought you'd be glad of the opportunity to boast,' she said, trying to sound cool. Which was far from her real temperature at that moment.

'You think I've had so many, then? What makes you think that?' She found herself unable to look away from those bright, piercing, laughing eyes.

'You're that sort of man,' she said helplessly, giving up the attempt to explain. 'Some women find your sort of looks and manner attractive.'

There was a tightness to her throat, a shiver down her spine, that had nothing to do with the cool sea.

'Tell me about my looks, then,' Zoltan invited, his voice a deep purr as he drifted up to her. She opened her mouth to make some flippant retort—and found she couldn't.

Oh, he was so handsome, those wonderful eyes seeming to reach deep into her brain, seeing all, understanding all.

'Tongue-tied?' he murmured. 'Then let me tell you about your looks, Rose. You're as gentle as the dove, as beautiful as the dawn . . .' She cried out, low in her throat as his arms found her, pulling her close against him. 'Your eyes are deep and soft, your skin like Burmese silk. You make me want you, dark-eyed Rose. You make me want you so much . . .'

Her naked stomach brushed against his, flinching. Like a drowning woman, she clung to him as his mouth descended on hers. Her body was terrifyingly aware of his warmth, the power of his thighs, the mystery of his loins against hers. His lips were cool on her mouth, and she surrendered helplessly to his kiss. Her blood surged in her veins like freshly-unbottled champagne, singing in her ears and racing through her body.

He was so fierce, so possessive! There was an authority in his mouth that quelled her utterly, frightened her; and then, slowly, their kiss deepened into a sharing, a unity that was like nothing she had ever known.

Suddenly frightened by the intensity of her own feelings, she tried to break away from him.

'Zoltan, no——'

'Are you hoisting up your petticoats again?' he growled. '*J'en ai assez!*'

And he crushed her to him, his mouth forcing her to respond. Her breasts taut against his chest, her legs imprisoned by a horseman's potent thighs, Rose felt herself about to disintegrate, a block of ice that some child had thrust into a furnace.

There was a moment of chaos inside her, a primaeval confusion that twisted her heart and strained her body and then, without thoughts or conscious will, she was responding to him, her own arms sliding around his neck to bring him closer, her hands feverishly caressing the thick wet tangle of his hair.

The sea cradled them, the dark, ancient cradle of all life, as they kissed, their mouths fusing into one flame, one furnace.

Zoltan's hands caressed urgently down her flanks, moulding the swell of her hips, and drawing her tight against him.

With a heart-stopping shock, she felt the surge of his desire naked against her, a force that melted her very bones and made her soul faint within her. Her lips opened unresistingly to his kiss. Now no water could cool her, no darkness hide her from him. Her fingers knotted in his wet hair, her long lashes shut tight over her eyes.

Keeping one hand against the small of her back, pressing her to him, Zoltan caressed the wet satin of her side, his fingers sliding up to touch the soft curve of her breast.

A deep, long shudder went through her as he cupped her breast, finding the unbearably tense peak, offering it the release of a harsh caress. Electricity seemed to jolt inside her, and she began to shiver uncontrollably.

Slowly, agonisingly slowly, he slid away from her. Her lips clung to his, refusing to be parted from him; but at last he drew back, his arms still supporting her. She opened her dazed eyes. That warm power, the intoxicating thrust of his loins, had been taken away from her.

'I'm glad that our first kiss was in the sea,' he said, the caress in his voice making her shudder again. 'My poor Rose, you're shivering!'

'I'm cold,' she whispered.

'Then let's go ashore. There's some *raki* at the cottage—and we can light a fire.'

'But our clothes——' she protested weakly as he led her towards the beach.

'After what's just passed between us, do we have any need for clothes?' he smiled, his eyes bright. 'There are towels in the cottage, and perhaps some dry beach-robes. You should be able to feel the bottom now.'

She lowered her trembling legs slowly. Her questing toes met the fine sand of the bottom. His fingers locked in hers, Zoltan led her through the gentle breakers, and they waded ashore, naked in the moonlight.

The air was warm on her wet, bare skin, but her knees were so weak that she thought she was going to stumble for a second.

'All right?'

'Yes,' she nodded, glad to feel dry sand under her feet. Covertly she glanced at Zoltan. He was superb in the moonlight, a flawless animal whose nakedness was proud, virile. Catching her eyes on him, he smiled.

'You grow bold, my dear Rose. An hour ago you would have been studiously averting those soft brown eyes.' His own gaze washed over her figure, dwelling with shameless male attention to her breasts and legs. 'I thought your body would be like every other female body I've seen,' he said softly, 'but I was wrong. You're more beautiful, more sweetly feminine——' For a dizzy second, Rose thought he was going to kiss her again. She tugged her fingers loose from his, and covered her breasts with her hands, in an age-old gesture of feminine modesty.

'Don't look at me like that,' she pleaded. Suddenly she was hotly, madly shy.

'Rose, Rose,' he sighed, his smile wry. 'You weren't ashamed in the water. Why be ashamed now?'

'I just am!' she said. 'Please let's get into the house.'

'We won't get there with your eyes shut,' he said with a gurgle of laughter. And indeed, she found that her eyes were tightly shut against that male beauty.

'Please!' she said again, her voice desperate.

'Come on, then,' he smiled, respecting her wishes. 'The chastest way will be arm-in-arm, I think.' She flinched as she felt the velvet skin of his muscular arm take hers. 'Now open your eyes.'

Gingerly she obeyed.

'Now,' he said solemnly, 'if we both keep our eyes

fixed firmly ahead, neither of us will see anything to corrupt or shock ourselves. Agreed?'

'I guess you think I'm ridiculous,' she muttered as they made their way to the stairs across the soft sand.

'You're not ridiculous, Rose,' he told her quietly. 'In fact, I find your modesty rather delicious.'

'Oh,' she said, and concentrated on not turning her head.

Ten minutes later she emerged from a luxurious bathroom, combing out her long hair with a woman's comb (a stab of jealousy had accompanied finding it) that had been in the wall-cabinet. She was wrapped in a towelling robe at least three sizes too big for her—but it was bliss to be clothed again.

'Is this what you call a beach cottage?' she asked in awe, looking around the beautiful living-room. It was tiled in marble, covered with rough Turkish rugs, one huge room that was luminous with huge windows looking out over the moonlit sea. During the day, she guessed, this would be a dazzling, beautiful place to live. Now, looking out over the white yacht on the wine-dark water below, it was magical, mystical. They hadn't bothered with the oil-lamps; the moonlight was soft and bright, and the fire that Zoltan was building was now adding its own red glow.

She nestled into an armchair and watched him nurturing the fire. The fireplace was a rough stone altar in the centre of the room. An ultra-modern flue directly above it led to the chimney, allowing no fumes to escape. On the dark slate was a single great log, its orange glow now breaking into blue-and-yellow flames under Zoltan's persuasion.

'You like it?'

'I've never seen anything like it. You must be very wealthy, Zoltan.'

'I'm able to indulge my tastes,' he smiled.

'And it all comes from investments on the stock market?' she asked.

'I'm a financial genius,' he said modestly. Rose smiled. He was so beautiful physically that she sometimes forgot the razor-sharp brain that lived behind those stunning eyes.

The log was crackling now, the warmth of its combustion sending languorous fingers through Rose's wet hair. Zoltan took glasses and a bottle from a cabinet.

'*Raki*,' he informed her. 'Bottled lightning.' He passed her a glass of the pale liquor, and smiled down at her, mysterious in his dark-blue robe. 'To you, Rose. *Salut*.'

The sweet, anise-flavoured alcohol burned its way down, exotic and pungent. Rose lay back with a sigh. Zoltan walked to the window and stared out into the moonlight, his glass cradled in both hands.

'Was that the first time you've kissed a man like that?' he asked quietly. She froze, then nodded slowly.

'Yes,' she said, her voice barely audible.

'It wasn't hard to tell.'

'Was I so clumsy?' she enquired with a touch of bitterness. He half turned, giving her a glimpse of his profile, the firelight flickering on the contours of his cheek.

'Clumsy? No. No more clumsy than a bud unfolding. Or a nightingale trying out her first songs.' He glanced up at the sky. 'Round here they say that the moon is a lamp, by which the nightingales sit late, studying their music.' He smiled briefly. 'No, Rose, you aren't clumsy.' He turned to face her, drinking from his glass. 'To tell the truth, I find you fascinating. Intriguing.'

'Me?' she asked, trying to sound a lot more flippant than she felt. 'You must have known so many fascinating women, Zoltan.'

'Yes,' he acknowledged frankly, 'I won't deny that.'

'Then why do you find me so fascinating?' She gulped the raw spirit to steady her nerves. 'Because I'm so innocent? Like a bud unfolding?'

'Partly,' he nodded.

'The doe interests the tiger,' she said, staring into the pearly liquid in her tumbler. 'I see you're addicted to the excitement of the chase.' She smiled sadly up at him. 'And when you've made your kill, what then? Then all interest fades, and you live only for the next chase, the next kill.'

'No.' He shook his head, his eyes dark. 'Your mind is full of stereotypes, Rose. Don't try and label me—I don't try and label you.'

'Then why do you find me so fascinating?'

'For your own sake, you little idiot,' he said with a smile. 'Is that so extraordinary?'

She shrugged, looking away from his smile into the flames. But her heart was leaping with joy. Oh, she so wanted to believe him!

'Out there in the water you said that some women would find me attractive,' he said, a wicked glint in his eyes. 'You wouldn't by any chance be one of those women?'

'I had no idea that vanity was one of your flaws,' she said, to hide her confusion.

'Ah, I am more wicked than you could possibly imagine,' he purred. 'My sins are numbered in multitudes.'

'My stomach hurt for days after you hit me,' she said *à propos* nothing.

'Had I known what a stubborn little creature you were going to turn out,' he grinned. 'I might have hit a lot harder!' Then his face grew serious. 'Rose, you don't know how sorry I am about that. When you went sprawling in the snow, I was astounded. Your hood flew off, and your beautiful hair tumbled out. I had thought you were a boy, or a slight man. When I saw your beauty——' He stopped, and smiled. 'You can imagine my feelings.'

'I wish you could imagine mine,' she said with a grimace.

'Your face stayed in my mind for weeks after that, Rose. I couldn't get your image out of my brain.'

'Huh,' she smiled, 'you didn't even recognise me when I turned up in your corridor!'

'You were different then—sophisticated, tidy. Not the dark-eyed girl with the tumbled hair and an Afghan coat.' Thoughtfully, Zoltan gulped at the *raki*. 'That operation in the hills was both boring and dangerous, Rose. There were many moments of peril, hours of hardship. Through it all, I kept your face close to my heart. You comforted me when I was cold and afraid, spurred me on when I was in danger.' She watched him in wide-eyed silence. He looked up with a quick smile. 'You don't know the number of times I cursed myself for having struck you, for not having been able to explain what I was doing, why I deceived you.'

'I must admit,' she confessed, lowering her gaze, 'I said some harsh things about you, Zoltan.'

'It was a dramatic introduction,' he nodded, a slow smile curving his sensuous lips. 'And in its way, a fitting way to begin such a turbulent relationship. I believe the original inhabitants of those caves used similar courtship methods.'

She shared his smile.

'You're no Neanderthal man,' she said. 'I've never known anyone quite so complex—or sophisticated—as you.' She leaned her head back against the cushion. 'How did a Frenchman happen to fall in love with a Hungarian girl?'

'Ah,' he smiled, his eyes losing their bright focus as he gazed into himself. 'That was in the bad days after the war. My mother was a refugee in London. She and her family had fled to England in the early weeks of Hitler's invasion. Her father was killed in the Resistance. When the war was over, she went to Paris with some friends for a weekend. My father saw her face through the train window at the Gare du Nord, and leaped on to the train to find her.'

'How romantic!' she laughed, fascinated.

'I'm afraid his family waited for him in vain that afternoon. He and my mother spoke barely a word of each other's language—yet they fell in love at once.'

'Like in the movies?'

'Like in those old black-and-white movies,' Zoltan agreed with a smile. 'They were married a week later. I was born in Normandy in the following year, my sister two years after that.'

'You've got a sister?'

'Claudette,' he nodded. 'She's a nurse in Paris. Happily married to an adoring husband, with three fat babies.'

'Does she look like you?' Rose asked impulsively.

'A little,' he nodded in surprise. 'We have the same colouring—although she is much prettier than I, of course.'

'She must be truly beautiful,' Rose said softly. She hesitated. 'And—and the babies?' she asked—as though through his sister's children she could catch some glimpse of what his own children would look like.

'Babies are babies,' he smiled. 'Barely a year separates them. They're black-haired, red-cheeked French babies, horribly spoiled by an adoring family, and precocious to the point of driving everybody crazy. Why the interest?'

'No reason,' she said. 'Are your parents still alive?'

'My mother died when we were still children,' he said gently, his grey eyes soft now, as though remembering some distant pain. 'My father was lost in a yachting accident two years ago. It was the way he would have chosen to die—in the arms of the sea.' He drank thoughtfully. 'In a way, my father was only half alive after my mother's death. He looked after Claudette and me, saw us through university and into adulthood. But we all knew secretly that he was just waiting to be with Maman.'

Rose sat in silence, watching the emotions playing across his face in the firelight.

'They were truly in love, those two,' he said under his breath. 'They had something that went beyond life, beyond everything. I don't think they ever stopped talking to one another, not even after Maman died.'

'You loved them both,' she said, her question almost a statement.

'Yes,' he nodded slowly. 'I love them still. So does Claudette.' He looked up, the fire glowing in his eyes. 'You're very inquisitive all of a sudden, Rose.' He came over to her, and passed her his glass. 'More *raki*. It warms the stomach after a swim.'

Obediently, she took the glasses over to the cabinet and poured them both another drink. She had been fascinated by this glimpse into Zoltan's private life. Somehow, it had thrown him into perspective, adding warmth and humanity to the profound attraction he exerted over her.

'The sun will be up soon,' he said, sitting down in one of the luxurious armchairs. She brought him his drink, and he took it with a smile.

Not wanting to be too far from him, Rose sat on the thick wool carpet at his knees and sipped the rich anise liqueur.

'I'm having a group of friends to lunch at my house tomorrow,' Zoltan told her. 'Sarai will be there, and Andreas Jacobi, a colleague. Will you come?'

'Yes,' she answered without hesitation. 'Tell me more about your childhood.'

'My childhood?' He smiled. 'I fought with my sister, climbed trees, sailed boats, loved a succession of mongrel dogs. What else do boys do?'

'Were you happy?'

'Blissfully. Until Maman died.' He changed the subject. 'And you? Were you a beautiful child with long tresses?'

'And grubby knees? I suppose so. I was very happy. But I guess I was a bit of an ordeal for Freddie. He's so much older than me. When I was a little girl, I thought my brother was the greatest thing in the world. I used to follow him everywhere, like a puppy. He never quite managed to shake me off, though I know he was dreadfully embarrassed in front of his friends.'

Zoltan smiled at the image. 'And when your parents died?' he prompted gently.

'It was as though the world had come to an end,' she said in a low voice. Without thinking, she laid her head against his knee, warm in the firelight. He stroked her hair, running his fingers slowly through the heavy curls. Hypnotised by the luxurious caress, Rose allowed her eyelids to droop closed.

'Freddie and I had nothing except each other,' she said dreamily. 'He was the most important thing in my life. Until he left for Chicago. And I met Barry.'

'Barry?'

'He was blond and handsome,' she sighed. 'Not like you—but I thought he was lovely.' She was silent for a while, adoring the warm pleasure of his fingers through her hair. 'I thought he was Mr Right. When I found out he felt the same, I was so very happy—happier than I'd been since Mum and Dad died, I think. Happier than I'd ever been. We got engaged. We were going to be married in the summer, and leave for Canada.'

'And then?' His voice was harsh.

'And then he fell in love with Beulah Gordon from Tennessee, an American he'd met through some friends. At first I refused to believe it. But when I did, my whole world caved in like a pack of cards . . .'

They sat in silence for a while, listening to the hiss and crackle of the fire. Then Zoltan's strong fingers tightened in her hair, pulling hard enough to hurt. She opened her eyes to meet his bright stare.

'I don't like to think of you with any other man,' he growled.

'That was a long time ago,' she smiled. 'Months and months. And I'm not with any man now.'

'Wrong,' he said gruffly. He leaned forward to kiss her full on the mouth, his lips rough and possessive. 'You're with me.'

Rose slid her arms around his neck, and he lifted her on to his lap, his arms tight around her waist.

'Got that?' he growled, his fierce eyes full of a smoky grey light.

'Got it,' she said a little breathlessly. The soft material of his robe had slipped open, and she put her hand timidly against his chest. The curls under her fingers were crisp, his skin warm and silky.

'Zoltan——'

'No questions,' he cautioned. His lips were warm and firm, and her own lips clung to his, as though unable to bear parting with them. 'Do you want to know what you do to me?' he asked, one eyebrow lifting in a quirk she knew so well. Close up, he was more attractive than she could possibly have imagined.

'Feel.' He slid her hand over his heart. She felt his hard nipple against her palm—and then, as she pressed against the firm muscles, she became aware of the steady pounding of his heart, a raw, primitive rhythm that communicated his desire for her more urgently than any words. With a little gasp she folded against him, her own heart almost failing her. His fingers found the soft pulse at her throat, measured the wild flutter of her own emotions.

'Yes,' he said softly, 'you feel it too.'

'Zoltan,' she whispered, 'I'm new to all this. I—I don't know——'

'There is nothing to know,' he said, silencing her with a finger against her lips. 'And we have a visitor— look.'

Dreamily she raised her head. The sky was suffused with a rosy flush, and the first red spark of the sunrise was visible behind the yacht that waited on the sea below them.

Dawn with Zoltan. It was as beautiful as a dream, more beautiful in that it was real, would never fade away. Whatever happened between them, she would always have these precious memories to cherish.

And there was an aura that seemed to surround them, an intensely sweet atmosphere that told her these hours were unique in her life, special and almost overwhelmingly important.

An aura that told her she was falling in love with Zoltan, as surely as the sun was rising out of the sea.

Love? What did it mean? Was it this swelling inside the heart, this feeling that your very soul was going to burst with joy? Or was it the knowledge, deep inside her mind, this understanding that was growing inside her, minute by minute, hour by hour?

'You're in one of your trances again,' he said softly, kissing her eyelids. 'Are you happy?'

'Yes,' she whispered truthfully, 'blissfully happy. And you?'

'You'd make any man blissful,' he said, caressing her face. 'Yes, I'm happy, Rose. I've never been happier.'

She looked up at him with dreamy eyes. 'Do you mean that?'

'You ought to know without asking,' he reproved

her. 'Are you glad you decided to come here last night?'

'I wouldn't have missed it,' she sighed, 'for the world. I suppose you have work to get back to today? We couldn't just stay here for ever?'

'We'll come back,' he promised. 'Often. But I have to get going now, yes. Not because I want to.'

'I believe you,' she sighed. 'And I'm starving, if you don't mind the descent into practicalities. Are there any provisions in this palace?'

'Sure,' he smiled. 'Can you grill bacon and scramble eggs?'

'Of course.'

'Then I'll brew coffee.' He kissed her one last time, slow and lingeringly, and smiled into her eyes. 'We'd better get going,' he said gently, 'otherwise we might never leave.'

CHAPTER SIX

STARRY-EYED. Rose had always thought that expression a cliché; suddenly it had acquired a real meaning for her. When she looked at herself in the mirror, her eyes seemed brighter, softer than she had ever seen them before.

No—more than that. She felt starry *inside*, as though she were walking on clouds the whole time, way, way above the rest of humanity.

What the hell, she thought with a wry smile, it was impossible to put this feeling into words. The only phrases she could find were scraps of hackneyed old songs. She emerged into the sunlight from the labyrinthine darkness of the Market, clutching the engraved bronze coffee-pot she had bought.

How could you miss someone after only a day's separation? Yet she wasn't due to see Zoltan again till tomorrow, and she was already aching for his company. He had become a need in her, a kind of longing that seemed to pull her very heart out of shape.

Was this the way she had felt with Barry? The awful truth was that she could scarcely remember! Her affair with Barry had suddenly been dwarfed, become as remote as an incident from someone else's life. But she couldn't believe that she'd ever gone through this all before. You couldn't feel this twice.

Maybe now was the time to put on the brakes.

She found a street-corner stall and treated herself to a delicious cup of scalding tea, served in a little glass, mingling easily with the groups of excited tourists. Many, she could see, were Pakistanis and Arabs who had made the pilgrimage to the holy places in this holy city.

Was now the time to put on the brakes? There were trains and boats and planes leaving Istanbul every hour of the day for every destination under the sun. Should she slip on to one, and simply disappear?

Cowardly thoughts. But I am a coward, she thought with candour. Emotions as strong as this do frighten me. He's so strong, so clever—and I scarcely know where I am with him. If we did become lovers, and he left me——

She leaned back against the sunlit wall, brooding. It was like being drunk. Drunk with no ill-effects. You just couldn't think straight, couldn't wipe the silly smile off your face . . . There was so much to admire about him. That book, for example. He had given her three rough-draft chapters of his book about the Etruscans to read, and she had been riveted by every word. It wasn't just that his style was so lucid and precise, yet so subtle; Zoltan Stendhal wrote from deep knowledge and a real love for his subject. He had made the Etruscans come alive for her as never before. In those brief chapters she had felt herself part of their lost world, sharing in their secret civilisation . . .

Yes, he was a writer of power and brilliance, a man whose superb mind had taken him to the very highest levels of his profession. It was hard to believe that he could really be interested in her, a young stranger who had read his books at university. Incredible though it was, however, he really seemed to want her. He had, at least, treated her with a kindness and warmth that couldn't be interpreted in any other way. A surge of gratitude and pride touched her heart; let this not be another mirage, she prayed; let this be real.

But could you handle it if it *was* real? She had no answer to that lingering inward doubt. Zoltan was capable of stealing her heart in a thousand ways. It was a potent combination. Maybe too potent for her to deal with.

Maybe not.

Only time was going to tell. And those boats and trains and planes? Rose stirred herself, and wandered up the street with a faint smile, enjoying the bustle. Not yet. There was too much warmth in his eyes. Warmth for her. Promises in Zoltan's kisses, promises in his touch. He wanted her, he had made that intoxicatingly plain. Maybe in time he might feel more than simply desire.

He must, she thought with quiet urgency, he must, he must!

Because the feeling in her heart was more than simple desire. Much, much more.

Rose watched the peacock strut slowly under the thicket of trees. Beautiful bird, beautiful garden. She was standing beside the ruined mosque, half covered by a tangle of larches, spruces and firs, at the bottom of Zoltan's garden. As she watched, the peacock paused, then slowly spread its stunning tail, a vast fan of turquoise and ultramarine eyes set against a red-gold tapestry of feathers. The iridescent colours glowed in the dappled sunlight.

The dinner party Zoltan had asked her to attend was turning out to be a delightful occasion. And it was bliss to be with him again, and feel those deep grey eyes on her. His presence was a warmth that enveloped her deliciously, securely . . .

She glanced up at the little group strolling along the paved path ahead of her. Among them, Zoltan was so tall, so imposing! He turned back to look at her, a smile on that dazzlingly handsome face.

'Daydreaming? Come on.'

'I stayed to watch the peacock,' she called, walking up to them.

'The bird of love,' Sarai Murat said, and from under her sooty lashes, sent an arch look at the Belgian Count.

'*Ah, oui,*' the Count nodded, his expression adoring. He pressed the knob of his malacca cane against his moustache, gazing at Sarai with soft blue eyes.

Rose had to turn away to hide her smile. The Belgian Count, portly, middle-aged and balding, had obviously been smitten by Sarai's charms as if by a thunderbolt. There was something of the amorous walrus in his efforts to please the dark-eyed dancer, and the coquettish way she treated him could be most amusing.

'Only Zoltan would think of keeping peacocks in his garden,' Andreas Jacobi smiled. The third member of the lunch party, Andreas was a slight, blinking man with a pleasant, rounded face. Rose had liked him at once—there was something innocent in his smile, something boyish in the untidy curls of his brown hair. Like Zoltan, he was an archaeologist, and a junior lecturer at the American College.

'I've never seen a garden quite like it,' Rose sighed, looking around. It was a magical place, with its romantic ruin, archways open to the blue sky, and its great tangles of wild roses and rhododendrons, perfuming the air with scent. 'I love the wildness of it.'

'You should have seen it when I first bought the place,' Zoltan commented. 'I don't think a gardener had set foot in here since the time of the Sultans.' Casually, he took her arm, and she thrilled to the power of his muscles against her body.

She was wearing grey slacks tucked into an old and much-loved pair of supple leather boots, having been warned that Zoltan's parties were seldom formal affairs, and was rather proudly showing off an exquisitely-embroidered Persian jacket she had bought the day before in the Market. Zoltan himself, splendid in snug-fitting black jeans and a black polo-neck sweater, smiled down at her.

'I wouldn't have thought you were the type to like wild gardens, Rose. You struck me more as a flowerbed-and-lawn sort of person.'

'I'm sure Rose has her moments,' Andreas Jacobi defended her, and Sarai nodded.

'Indeed. Rose might almost be Turkish sometimes.'

'You think so?' Zoltan murmured, his bright grey eyes caressing Rose. 'I've noticed that myself. And in that beautiful jacket, she could be a Sultan's concubine.'

The double meaning in his words sent a dash of colour into Rose's cheeks.

'The light of the harem?' she suggested playfully. 'I'm far too selfish for that, I'm afraid. I should want to have my Sultan all to myself.'

'Bravo!' said the Belgian Count, but no one paid him any attention.

'Rose is Western to her soul,' Andreas Jacobi laughed. 'And so am I. I agree with you, Rose—all this Oriental herding of women into harems and veils offends my taste.'

'You Americans are always so quick to judge our Eastern ways,' said Sarai. She sent the Belgian Count another thunderbolt of a look from under her lashes, and like clockwork, the knob of his cane rose to tap his greying moustache.

'*Magnifique*,' he murmured, '*vraiment une Sirène*.'

'You don't mean to say that you, of all people, approve of *purdah*?' Andreas demanded.

'We do not practise *purdah* in Turkey, as you well know,' Sarai retorted. 'In fact, Turkish women are as free and as unrestricted as women in any Western country.' She nestled up to the Belgian Count. 'We simply choose to let our men be our lords,' she purred. 'And that shows how deeply feminine we are.'

'*Absolument*,' agreed the Count, his blue eyes earnest. 'Sarai is—oh, so feminine!'

'I can see that,' Andreas Jacobi grinned. 'But Rose here is feminine too—and you couldn't see her being contented in a harem, could you?'

'Besides,' Zoltan said silkily, 'all that stuff about Turkish women letting their men be their lords is just propaganda, *n'est-ce pas*, Sarai? That's just for public consumption. In the privacy of the *boudoir*, things are different. Many a swaggering Turkish husband in the street becomes a cowering, henpecked mouse in the bedroom!'

'You are horrible,' Sarai pouted through the general chuckle. 'You Frenchmen are all alike!'

'I'm half Hungarian,' Zoltan reminded her with a smile.

'Half Hungarian, half a devil,' Sarai quoted. 'I've told you to beware, Rose!'

'I'll try and remember,' Rose nodded solemnly. It was very sweet to walk at Zoltan's side like this, feeling his warm male presence next to her. What would life be like with this power, this wonderful man, always at her side?

She had been surprised to notice that, by daylight, Sarai Murat was a lot older than she had imagined. The cat-like face was well lived in, and the laughter lines around those slanting eyes showed that this magnificent body was inhabited by a woman who loved life and who enjoyed it to the full. It was with a sense of faint surprise that Rose calculated Sarai's age to be not less than thirty-six or seven. Sarai simply seethed with Oriental sex appeal—but despite that, Rose found her a captivating and genial person, with not a shred of malice in her make-up.

'Where did this half-devil take you after your

evening at Suleiman's Garden House, Rose?' Sarai was asking.

'Oh, we had such a lovely swim,' Rose told her. 'We went up to the Black Sea in Zoltan's yacht, and swam till the dawn.'

'*Ah, oui?*' said the Belgian Count, tapping his moustache with a thoughtful cane. 'But how *romantique*!'

Rose noticed Andreas Jacobi's eyes on her. Their expression was intense, dark. A faint look of concern passed over his face as he looked from her to Zoltan, but he said nothing. Puzzled, Rose turned to Sarai, who was laughing.

'Aha, my dear Rose! I thought I could see stars in your eyes that night.'

'Oh, nothing—happened,' she said hastily, aware of what the others might be thinking. 'We just swam and talked——' Conscious of sounding gauche, she stopped, blushing.

'It'll be time for lunch soon,' Zoltan cut gently through her embarrassment. 'Evliya has put on a special effort today. Shall we wander slowly back to the house?'

Rose fell into pace beside Zoltan as the other three walked on ahead. The black clothes made him dramatic, elegant, where they would have made a lesser man merely flamboyant.

'Your garden really is beautiful,' she said. 'It's like something from the Arabian Nights, with that mosque, and the peacocks.' As if echoing her sentiments, the harsh cry of one of the peacocks drifted up from the bottom of the garden. Zoltan slipped his arm through hers, drawing her closer, and making her heart skip a beat.

'Do you like Sarai on better acquaintance?' he asked.

'Yes,' she said firmly. 'She's so full of joy and life. The Count is rather funny, though.'

'Yes,' he nodded with a faint smile. 'Yet he obviously cares a great deal for her. And that somehow prevents one from laughing at him. Look.' Up ahead of them, the Count was presenting a flower to Sarai with stately affection while Andreas wandered along a flower-bed. Sarai patted his cheek, and they put they heads close together.

'Sarai has had so many men that I tend to lose track of them all,' said Zoltan, his body moving smoothly next to Rose's side. 'But it looks as though she's going to marry this one.'

'He's a lot older than she is,' Rose said dubiously.

'Sarai's no spring chicken. That beautiful body won't be dancing for ever. One day, the muscles will start to ache, and she'll grow weary of the stage and the music of the *tambur*. Emile's a good man, and in her way I think she loves him. They'll make a very stable, happy, fulfilled partnership,' he judged. Rose nodded. His intuition was perfect. Sarai and the Count were perfectly matched.

'You're right,' she smiled. 'As usual!'

'My only regret is that he'll almost certainly take her off to Europe. Can't you just see her, the Countess Sarai, being gracious in some mansion?'

'Yes,' Rose giggled. 'I wonder what the Countess Sarai's guests would say if they could have seen her at the Garden House of Suleiman the Red, dancing in a transparent veil?'

'It doesn't bear thinking of,' Zoltan agreed with a chuckle. 'I'm very happy for her—and for him. He's a sweet old boy.'

'You really care, don't you?' said Rose, looking up at him almost shyly.

'Why shouldn't I care about my friends?' he asked with a lift of one eyebrow. 'Do you think me a monster?'

'No,' she smiled. 'But it's a little difficult to

associate such a—well, such a *masculine* man with sentimental things.'

'Sentiment, not sentimentality,' he corrected her gently. 'The two are quite different. I value the people who are close to me.' His eyes were on hers as he spoke, and something in them made her heart flip backwards. She looked hastily down at the lush grass, wondering if he had any idea what he did to her.

'You must have many friends,' she prompted.

'Many acquaintances,' he replied. 'As for true friends, I can count them on the fingers of one hand.'

'You're exaggerating, surely,' she smiled.

'No,' he replied seriously. 'Do you have more than five friends who really know you, whom you truly love?'

'No,' she said, after a second's thought. 'But that's different. I've always been solitary. And I haven't met many people. Whereas you—you're glamorous, famous. People crowd around you.'

'You flatter me, little Rose,' Zoltan said softly. He laced his fingers through hers, his hand strong and warm against her palm. 'I'm a traveller, Rose—a gypsy. One of the prices you have to pay when you travel a lot is to accept that your friendships are limited. I don't think there are many people who really know me. Maybe there are none. I'm not a man who opens readily, *chérie*. And curiosity tends to make me positively oyster-like.'

'I've brought your chapters back,' she said, and hesitated, a little too in awe of him to tell him what she had thought of them. He glanced at her.

'Did you enjoy them?'

'You write extremely well. I'd forgotten how well.' Then, impulsively, she added, 'I thought what you said was fascinating, Zoltan. I don't think I've ever been so gripped by a piece of archaeological puzzle-solving.' Feeling foolish in the face of his quiet smile, she twisted her hands. 'You really re-created the world of the Etruscans. I had the feeling of being there. I don't know if you know what I mean—I had the feeling that everything you were saying, even your guesswork, was true. As though you'd actually been there in some kind of time machine, and had come back to report.'

'I have been there,' he said, that intriguing upward slant in his eyes deepening. 'In my mind. It's more guesswork than you imagine, Rose. But I'm glad you found it realistic.'

'More than realistic—vivid. I'm dying to read the next sections.' Again she hesitated. 'That vividness, that immediacy—it's the greatest quality an archaeological writer can have. At least, that's what I think,' she added, embarrassed by his laughter.

'I hope my publishers feel the same way,' he replied, his fingers tight around hers.

'Have they seen what you've written so far?'

'Mmm. They're clamouring for more.'

'I bet they are! I suppose you're one of their top sellers?'

'Archaeology isn't anyone's top seller,' he said wryly. 'It's a specialist subject, and very few people ever reach a wider public. People are slowly becoming more interested in the past, though. And I'm lucky, in that for some reason they keep buying my books.'

'It's more than luck,' Rose chided gently. 'What are you going to call this one?'

'*The Etruscan Darkness*,' he smiled. 'Dramatic, but effective, I think.'

A shout from Sarai drew their attention, and they looked up. She was holding some small prickly object, her cat-like face shining with delight.

'She's found a hedgehog,' Zoltan grinned. 'I wonder if she knows they're crawling with parasites?'

'I think Andreas is pointing that out to her right

now,' Rose said, watching the trio. 'He seems a very inoffensive, innocuous sort of person.'

'Andy? You think so?'

'He's pleasant,' Rose judged. 'He looks like the public image of a true archaeologist, doesn't he—mild, studious, reserved.'

'And yet Andy has a soul,' Zoltan said obliquely. She glanced up at him, but he was plucking a rhododendron flower.

'It's the season for flower-giving,' he said, pinning the purple blossom in her lapel. His touch, even through her clothes, sent a tingle through her body. Without warning, he leaned forward and kissed her lips firmly.

'You look ravishing in that embroidery,' he said, his eyes deep on hers. 'You should always wear rich clothes, Rose. They suit your beauty. The man who marries you will have to lap you in silk and deck you with pearls.' He kissed her again, this time on the temple, inhaling the smell of her hair. 'You smell sweet,' he murmured. 'Of myrrh and ambergris.'

Dizzily, she swayed against him.

'Zoltan,' she whispered, 'you don't know what happens to me when you talk like that. You mustn't.'

'Why not?' He looked down at her, his pupils dark and wide, leaving just a silver rim round his eyes. 'Saying these things doesn't offend you, does it?'

'No,' she said, smiling a little. 'But I might just take them seriously.'

'And you don't think I take you seriously?' he asked. The others were hidden from view behind a clump of golden laurel, and he took her in his arms under the trees and kissed her softly on both eyelids. 'My sweet Rose,' he said huskily, 'you don't know how serious I am about you.'

She closed her eyes as his lips brushed the corners of her mouth, then met her full on the lips. She could feel the sculpted hardness of his body against her, his mouth exploring hers with a tenderness that melted her bones and made her want to sink into the lush grass, clinging to him.

Slowly he drew away, leaving her dewy-eyed.

'We mustn't be rude to our guests,' he said gently. 'Can we resume this conversation later on, when we're alone?'

'Yes,' she whispered, still giddy.

'There's so much we have to say,' he said, his voice velvety, his eyes unfathomable. 'I wonder if we'll ever find the time?'

'We'll make the time,' she said breathlessly, drinking in every detail of his wonderful face with her eyes.

'Yes,' he nodded, stroking her cheek with his hand, 'we'll make the time.'

Her heart was singing as they walked up to rejoin the others. Singing a symphony that was still unfulfilled, still nervous—but brimming with a deep joy.

The lunch, served in the long dining-room, was a characteristically Turkish meal—delicious, leisurely, and consisting of an apparently limitless supply of different delicacies. To Rose's mingled delight and anxiety, Zoltan had placed her opposite him, as though she were to act as hostess. She did her best; and despite the odd number of guests—Andreas Jacobi was facing Sarai and her Count—the small party went off well.

Zoltan was the perfect host, urbane and attentive to his guests' needs, and he kept the conversation light and amusing. Towards the end of the meal, however, the Belgian Count—Rose never discovered his name—brought their host back to the subject of archaeology.

'I understand you are co-ordinating this *exposition*

archéologique, Zoltan, with the Americans?' he prompted over the dates and almonds cooked in honey.

'Yes. We're in the final stages of preparation right now.'

'What exhibition is this?' Rose wanted to know.

Zoltan glanced up at her with a quick smile.

'The American College and a number of other Turkish universities are contributing to a big exhibition of Middle Eastern Archaeology in New York next month,' he told her. 'I, for my sins, have been appointed as Director of the Turkish end.'

'Why play it down?' Sarai demanded. 'It's a great honour, *mon cher*.'

'Like many honours, it's also something of a penance,' Zoltan smiled. 'I don't know how I should have managed without Andreas. He's been invaluable.'

'Oh, I did nothing,' Andreas Jacobi blinked. His smile was hesitant, almost boyish, and again Rose found herself liking him instinctively. 'Imerely happened to have a little experience with packing precious objects for export, that's all.'

'What sort of things are you sending?' Rose asked.

'Some beautiful Assyrian statues,' Zoltan supplied. 'A good collection of armour and bronze weapons. Some silver and gold jewellery.'

'The best exhibits of all, to my mind, are the Sumerian vases,' Andreas put in. A loving smile of reminiscence spread over his face. 'Some truly exquisite pieces. But terribly fragile. We're going to pack them as best we can, of course—but I pray nothing gets broken. It's a long way to New York.'

'Where are the exhibits now?' the Count wanted to know.

'They're safe enough,' Zoltan said obliquely, but Andreas grinned.

'As a matter of fact,' he chuckled, 'they're right beneath you.' The Belgian Count examined the carpet below his feet in astonishment, and Rose caught the angry glance that Zoltan threw Andreas Jacobi.

'Don't look so cross, Zoltan,' Andreas smiled. 'I'm sure none of our friends will breathe a word.' He leaned forward to the other three. 'We racked our brains for a safe place to keep all these treasures—and eventually I hit on it. Zoltan's cellar! Like most old Turkish houses,' he explained, 'this place has an extensive underground store-room dating back to the Middle Ages. We came down and had a look—it was dry, clean, secure. The ideal place, in fact.'

'So we're sitting on a gold mine?' Sarai smiled.

'Not exactly,' Zoltan shrugged. 'The pieces aren't worth very much in intrinsic terms. Maybe a few hundred dollars. Archaeologically, though, they have an incalculable value.'

'True,' Andreas agreed. 'Some of the finest discoveries of recent years are there, waiting to be crated and shipped off to the U.S.A. The packing starts in a day or two.' He sipped from his coffee cup, blinking happily. 'Say, why don't we go down and take a look at the exhibits after lunch?'

'I don't think so,' Zoltan said quietly.

'Ah, Zoltan, *s'il vous plaît*,' Sarai pleaded. 'I should love to see the jewellery.'

'Yes, don't be such a stickler for rules,' Andreas urged with his boyish smile. 'There are some lovely things——'

'It isn't a very good idea,' Zoltan said gently, his smile firmly in place.

'But I'd be so interested to see the exhibits,' Rose put in. 'After all, at Igdir I——'

'I have already said no,' Zoltan cut through her sentence. His voice was soft, but stung like a silk lash. The diamond light in his grey eyes pierced Rose like a rapier. She sat back, slightly stunned by the raw will-power in the man. There was a puzzled silence. Andreas Jacobi blinked down at his plate.

'Those items are extremely precious,' Zoltan continued more gently. 'And I'm personally responsible for them. I couldn't take the chance of anything happening to them.'

'Of course, of course, *mon vieux*,' the Belgian Count said soothingly. 'We quite understand.'

'Now,' Zoltan went on, 'let's forget archaeology. I dislike talking shop on social occasions. 'Let's have some more coffee in the drawing-room. And perhaps we can persuade Sarai to do a little fortune-telling.'

'Do you tell fortunes?' Rose asked as they all rose, eager to smooth over the awkward spot in the conversation.

'A little,' Sarai smiled. 'I read the *tarok*.'

'The Tarot cards?'

'Exactly. A lot of old gypsy nonsense, of course,' the dancer deprecated.

'I'm not so sure of that,' Zoltan smiled, ushering them into the beautiful study. 'I've known Sarai to be uncannily accurate on occasions.'

'Well, perhaps I have some slight gift,' Sarai admitted, not displeased. 'Have you some cards, Zoltan?'

'I think so. There should be a pack in this drawer. Yes, here.' He passed the cards over to the dark little dancer, and she riffled through them expertly.

'Now,' she smiled, 'whose fortune shall I read? Yours, Andreas?'

'No, thank you,' the young archaeologist said hastily. 'I don't want you finding out all my secrets, Sarai.'

'Emile, my dear?'

'Ah, no, *chérie*,' the Count said. 'I am far too superstitious for these games.'

Sarai pulled a face. 'I shan't try you, Zoltan—some Hungarian devil in you always manages to mix up the cards so that I can't see anything.' She turned her dark eyes on Rose. 'It will have to be you, *ma petite.*'

'With pleasure,' Rose smiled, sitting down in front of Sarai. 'What do I have to do?'

Zoltan's smoky grey eyes were on her as she shuffled and cut the deck according to Sarai's instructions. She was acutely conscious of his gaze, and of the slow smile that was curving on his passionate mouth. Being watched by Zoltan, as she was coming to discover very swiftly, was both a delight and a torment. A delight in that the woman in her thrilled to the knowledge that he desired her, was dwelling on her face and figure. A delight in that every time she looked up she met those stunning eyes, with their secret, heart-stopping message that was only for her.

But a torment in that his gaze made her stumblingly shy and selfconscious, continually afraid of doing something gauche or inelegant.

'Now,' said Sarai, her liquid brown eyes intent on the cards in Rose's slim fingers, 'what is it to be, Rose? Shall we lay out a spread of cards and tell your life-story? Or shall I predict your future on the strength of one mystical card?'

'I know all about my own past life,' Rose decided. 'Tell me about my future, Sarai.'

'Very well.' The sooty lashes were lowered over the Turkish woman's eyes, her face unusually solemn. A little shiver went through Rose. Perhaps this gay, sensual woman really did have some gypsy gift of second sight.

'Pick a card,' Sarai said softly.

Rose hesitated. Then, her eyes locked on Zoltan's, she drew a card slowly from the deck.

'Turn it over.'

Rose dropped the card on to the serpentine coffee-table, and dropped her eyes to it. The others were sitting back over their coffee, looking on.

'The Moon,' Sarai said quietly. She stared at the strange card for a while, her feline face strangely impassive.

'The Moon? What does that mean?' Rose asked anxiously.

'It's a strange card,' Sarai said unwillingly. 'It often means something which it doesn't say.'

'Don't be so obscure,' Zoltan commanded. 'What does it predict?'

Sarai drew a quick breath.

'This card implies deception,' she said expressionlessly. 'Also insincerity, dishonesty. An influence has come into your life recently—a dangerous influence. Someone who is not what he seems. Someone who is deceiving you, and who brings you unforeseen perils.'

'Deception?' Rose echoed blankly. 'Unforeseen perils? What does that mean? What kind of perils, Sarai?'

'If she could tell you that,' Zoltan said ironically, 'they wouldn't be unforeseen. Would they?'

'The card also may mean slander. Someone who comes out of the unknown.' She narrowed her eyes, groping after the words. 'I don't know how to put it—a person who is *équivoque. Déguisé.*'

'An ambiguous man,' Andreas Jacobi supplied thoughtfully. 'Someone in disguise.'

'Exactly,' Sarai nodded. The narrowed black eyes were fixed on Rose. 'You must beware, *ma petite.* Things are not always as they seem.'

A chill made Rose shiver suddenly. Noticing the gesture, Sarai swept the cards up with an exclamation of disgust.

'There, I have succeeded in frightening you. What a fool I am, Rose! Please, forgive me. It's all nonsense, stupidness. Forget it.'

'Someone in disguise,' Andreas said thoughtfully, his eyes drifting to Zoltan. 'Who can that be?'

'No—enough now,' Sarai begged. 'Let's enjoy ourselves and forget the whole thing. It was a stupid joke that went wrong.'

'But there is always a measure of truth in these jokes,' said the Count, his protruberant blue eyes solemn. 'That is why I never like to play with such things.'

'Ah,' Sarai sighed, rolling her eyes at him, 'you have such a sensitive soul, Emile. You feel things too much.'

Like a metronome, the Count's stick shot up to press amorously against his moustache.

'It is true,' he said, gazing adoringly at his companion. 'My heart is very tender. It was always so, even when I was a child.'

Zoltan's amused gaze met Rose's as the incongruous pair kissed with stately gallantry, and she smiled intimately at him.

But a little uneasy chill had settled in her stomach, a chill that was totally irrational, and very hard to shake off.

The moment passed away in conversation, but Rose was again aware of a concerned look in Andreas Jacobi's mild face—the same look she had intercepted earlier on.

Later in the afternoon, when Rose had strolled out alone on to the verandah to gaze out over the autumn tints in the garden below, Andreas followed her. Standing next to her, he blinked peacefully over the reds and golds of the trees.

'I love this time of year,' he murmured. 'So peaceful. As though Nature were winding up her affairs for the winter.'

Rose nodded. Andreas cleared his throat uncertainly, and glanced back through the French doors to where Zoltan was talking to Sarai and the Count.

'Rose——' he began tentatively, 'would you mind if I said something?'

'Go ahead,' she invited casually.

'You may not like it,' he warned, tugging at his lower lip anxiously. 'And you'd be well within your rights to curse me sideways for not minding my own damn business——'

She glanced at the young archaeologist. His narrow, boyish face was showing a mixture of discomfort and determination, as though he were screwing up his courage to say something he didn't like saying. Her heart sank slightly, she didn't know why.

'Please go ahead,' she said in a low voice.

Andreas drew a deep breath.

'Well, when Sarai read your cards back there, it gave me quite a start. And I felt I just had to talk to you, even if it made you really mad at me. But you're such an innocent, sweet person, Rose. And I don't want you to be hurt.'

'By whom?' she asked quietly. 'By Zoltan?'

'I'm afraid so,' he said with a twist to his immature mouth. 'Look, I know Zoltan Stendhal's a great archaeologist, a brilliant scholar. It's been a privilege to have him in control of this project, to work with someone so dedicated——'

'But?' said Rose in the pause, biting back her anger.

'But I have to tell you that Zoltan's no fit companion for someone like you, Rose. You're very trusting, and—if you'll forgive me—a little inexperienced in the ways of men. This is going to hurt, Rose—but Zoltan happens to be a ladykiller *par excellence*.'

'I see,' she said in a low voice. There was compassion in Andreas Jacobi's eyes—and for once, they had stopped their usual nervous blinking.

'In fact, he's notorious. Women seem to find him

irresistible, and he capitalises on that. He's addicted to women the way some men are addicted to drugs.'

'And why are you telling me all this?' Rose asked steadily.

'Because I don't think you mean very much to Zoltan Stendhal. And by the way you look at him, I think he means a great deal to you.'

Rose dropped her eyes silently.

'He's not what you think he is, Rose.' Andreas' voice was gentle, but she could hear the sincerity in it. 'A lot of people have misjudged Zoltan. Underneath that civilised veneer, he can be an extremely dangerous man. Believe me.'

Rose leaned silently on the balustrade, fighting back the bitter, tearful retorts that were welling up inside her. In his gentle way, Andreas Jacobi was making the foundations of her world totter and sway, and the pain was tearing at her heart.

Why couldn't she simply tell Andreas that he was talking nonsense, turn and walk away? Was it because of the sincerity evident in his young face? Or because what he was saying touched on some inner suspicions of her own, suspicions she had long ago hidden and forgotten about? Biting her lip, she recalled the sudden violence of that blow high up in the hills of Agri.

Andreas touched her arm lightly.

'I'm sorry, Rose. But I just had to say that—I had to warn you to be careful, that's all. Maybe I've put it all a lot too harshly——'

'Oh, don't apologise,' she said with a touch of bitterness, her voice tight in her throat. 'I'm grateful for your concern. I suppose you've got some reason for saying all this?'

Andreas twisted his neck uncomfortably. 'I just want to warn you,' he said. 'I know Zoltan a lot better than you, don't forget. Oh, don't get me wrong—he's a brilliant archaeologist, I'm not disputing that. I've just been proof-reading the final sections of a new book he's written about the Etruscans, as a matter of fact—absolutely brilliant stuff. It's going to revolutionise the way people think about Etruscan history.'

'I know,' she said dully. 'I've read bits of it.'

'Then you know what an exceptional writer he is. But being brilliant at his work doesn't mean he has to be a very moral person. In my experience,' Andreas added with a hint of acid in his voice, 'it's actually rather the reverse.'

Rose mustered her miserable thoughts. 'You say he's dangerous. What do you mean by that?'

'Just what I say.' He blinked at her earnestly. 'You wouldn't be the first young woman to have her life destroyed by Zoltan Stendhal, Rose. Istanbul University is practically littered with girls who've had their hearts broken by him. I mean, with a face and figure like his, and with a brain like that—he's bound to find conquests easy, isn't he?'

'I guess so,' Rose mumbled, feeling her heart twist inside her.

'These very talented people are often like that,' Andreas went on gently. 'They have different standards from the rest of us. They're used to getting their own way, no matter what. And there are always queues of women waiting to oblige.' He glanced into Rose's eyes. 'I'm afraid Zoltan's one of those unscrupulous, highly-sexed men who——'

'Don't go on,' she interrupted, suddenly covering her ears and shutting her eyes. '*Please!*' After a while, she lowered her hands tiredly. 'Andreas, I don't know what to say——'

She broke off as Zoltan strolled out on to the verandah, his usual smile in place.

'Confidences?' he asked lightly, coming close to her

and taking her arm. She couldn't do anything about the thrill that his touch sent through her body.

'We were just saying how lovely the garden was looking,' she said, smiling up at him. But her eyes were dark with pain, and she ached for this magnificent dream-man over whom such a shadow had suddenly been cast.

'You looked very serious about it,' Zoltan said gently. His bright grey eyes glanced from Andreas' blinking face to Rose's pale cheeks. He was so beautiful, Rose thought in sudden anguish. Surely Andreas was wrong! It wasn't possible that so fair an exterior could be rotten within!

With a defiant glance at Andreas, she pulled close to him, her fingers trembling against the powerful muscles of his arms.

'Why, Rose,' he said in surprise, 'you're shaking. Are you cold?'

'It's the evening coming on,' she said with a weak smile.

'Come inside, then,' Zoltan urged. 'Evliya is making a fire, and you can toast your feet beside it.' He turned to Andreas. 'Andy, I'm going to drive Sarai and Emile back to Beyazit in a minute. Would you like a lift to the University?'

'That would be fine,' the younger man nodded. He gave Rose a smile in which compassion and concern were mingled, his weak eyes blinking uncertainly. Then he nodded, repeating, 'That would be fine,' and walked back into the drawing-room with them.

The young boy was lighting a log fire in the grate—it was truthfully colder now, and a chilly autumn evening would soon be closing in. The others were preparing to leave. Taking Rose aside, Zoltan looked piercingly into her eyes.

'Are you okay?' She stared up at him. In the black clothes, he was magnificent, dramatic. The jeans hugged his hips and thighs, emphasising the taut power in that virile body, and the silk polo-neck sweater clung to the swelling lines of his chest and arms. He was so beautiful that her heart ached for him.

'I'm fine,' she nodded, losing herself in the depths of his eyes.

'Sure?'

'Sure.'

Satisfied, he nodded. 'I'm driving Andy and Sarai and Emile back to town now. Will you stay and wait here for me? I want to have time alone with you for a while.' He stooped, making her dizzy with the softness of his kiss. Her lips clung to his as her fingers clutched at his arms. Then he drew back. 'Okay? I won't be more than half an hour, I promise.'

'I'll be waiting,' she promised. And I'll be counting every second as jealously as though it were another woman waiting to take you away from me, she added to herself. Don't be anything but what you are, Zoltan! Please God, don't let this turn out like Barry. I couldn't survive it this time . . .

Oblivious to the turmoil inside Rose, Zoltan turned away to round up his guests. Andreas Jacobi said a hurried goodbye in a low voice, his handshake a brief pressure. He and the Belgian Count walked with Zoltan out into the courtyard where the sleek grey car was parked.

Sarai hesitated for a minute, pulling black kid gloves on to her slim fingers.

'*Ma petite* Rose,' she said quietly, 'will you promise me to forget utterly that foolish nonsense I talked this afternoon?'

'Of course I will,' Rose smiled. 'It was just a game.'

'Exactly, just a game,' Sarai nodded. 'I didn't mean to upset you.'

'I wasn't upset,' Rose protested with another laugh.

'Weren't you?' The quick dark eyes were intelligent. 'I hope not, Rose. Some people take these things so very seriously. I don't.'

'Nor do I,' Rose assured her. 'You don't have to explain, Sarai.'

'Good.' Impulsively, the small woman darted a kiss on to Rose's cheek. 'You're a sweet person, Rose, a honey. And I think you and Zoltan are very lucky to have found one another.'

Rose flushed slightly, not knowing what to say.

'Zoltan is a man such as women dream of,' Sarai said softly, her full lips smiling tenderly. 'You cannot know how I envy you. Once upon a time, I too had such a man.' A bitter-sweet slant came into the smile. 'But, like the fool I am, I lost him. I lost the one man on earth whom I truly loved, Rose. And now I flit from one *affaire* to another, without hope, without real satisfaction . . .'

'*Chérie!*' The Count's voice drifted from the twilight outside, and Sarai pulled a wry face.

'Why is there never the time to say the things that really need saying?' she asked. 'I'll be one minute, Emile,' she called over her shoulder. She turned back to Rose. 'You like him?'

'He's very sweet,' said Rose.

'Yes. I shall probably marry him. He's kind, and gentle. But he's not . . .' Sarai paused, shrugged slightly, and patted Rose's cheek with a velvety palm. 'See that you do not lose your man, little one.'

'Sarai——' Rose began hurriedly, 'is Zoltan—is he a good man?'

'A good man?' Sarai smiled gently. 'In what way? If you mean good inside, good in his heart—yes. He may not conform to the goodness of strict religious people, the people who say all pleasure is bad. Zoltan is attractive to women, Rose, you must know that. But it seems to me that he thinks very highly of you. You may be sure that if he commits himself to you, little one, he will be as true as steel.'

'Is he intrinsically good?' she asked, twisting her hands.

'Listen,' Sarai said gently, looking into Rose's eyes steadily. 'Some time ago, I was very ill—ill almost to the point of dying. No one had the patience to put up with me, no one except Zoltan. He took me into his house, made me welcome. He nursed me as tenderly as—I would have said as tenderly as a woman, but that there is nothing of the woman in Zoltan's make-up. He is all man, *chérie*. A man to warm a woman's bed and fill her life with joy. That much I can tell you,' she smiled. 'More I do not know. There was never anything between us.' An inward light came into her slanted eyes. 'Not, I must confess, that I didn't desire it. You see how honest I am? But as for your confusion, your worries—well, you must work those out for yourself, Rose. No one can do that for you. I must fly now.' She squeezed Rose's hand. *'Au 'voir, chérie*—and *bonne chance!'*

Watching the full figure hurry off into the gathering dusk, Rose shook her head ruefully. Poor Sarai. She recalled Zoltan saying that she had led an unhappy life, and now she had a clue as to why.

As she stared at the receding tail-lights of Zoltan's car, Rose smiled a little bitterly to herself. Well, who was she to believe, Sarai or Andreas? She closed the door and strolled back to the study. Andreas' words echoed in her mind. *He's not what he seems to be.* A sharp pain made her wince.

Why couldn't she simply cast aside what Andreas had said as the ramblings of a young fool, or the petty jealousy of a lesser man? Really, she should have slapped his face!

But the concern, the compassion in the gentle, blinking face haunted her.

'Some coffee, *madame?*'

'No, thanks, Evliya,' she told the boy. 'I'll just sit by the fire until Zoltan comes back.'

'Very well, *madame.*' Smiling, he retreated, leaving her alone beside the crackling fire. A damp mist had begun to gather with the dying of the sun, and it was good to stand beside the resin-smelling heat indoors. She stared absently into the flames, pondering on what Andreas and Sarai had said to her.

Oh, Zoltan . . . If this ache in her heart, this fire in her soul were anything to go by, then she was falling in love. Irrevocably. A fragment of what Sarai had said drifted into her mind. *The one man on earth whom I truly loved . . .* Yes, she understood what that felt like. In all this wide world, only one man had ever touched her in this way.

And with a woman's deep instinct, she knew that no other man could ever touch her like this again. What Zoltan did to her was unique, a wonderful magic that made her something special in the universe. A feeling that transcended her, filled her with music and joy.

Again her thoughts returned to Barry. She had been so bitter, so tormented after that had ended. But why? What she and Barry had had was never anything to compare with this. And hadn't it been far better to see through Barry when she had, and not when it had become too late—say, after a marriage, maybe even children? She shuddered slightly. Had she but known it, Barry's defection with Beulah Gordon of Tennessee had been the narrowest escape of her life. It would have destroyed her altogether to have been bound to that shallow, uncaring man for the rest of her life. And instead, she was now on the brink of a new life, a new happiness, a future that held nothing but joy for her.

Poor Beulah, she thought, with a sudden sense of pity. I wonder if you're going to be able to make a man out of Barry. Somehow, she doubted it.

Hurry back, my darling! Restlessly, she stared round the room for something to occupy herself with, something to take her mind off the sweet agony of waiting for Zoltan. Her eyes were caught by the firelight glinting on something metallic lying on the serpentine coffee-table. Zoltan's ring of keys.

She picked the keys up, fingering them slowly. An idea struck her. Those exhibits for New York. Zoltan would surely not mind her going down to the cellar to take a look at them. His concern at lunch-time wouldn't extend to her, she was certain.

Picking up her bag, she walked out into the dark corridor, looking for the steps down to the lower level of the house.

The way down was easy enough. At the bottom of the stairs another long, dark corridor led to a heavy, brass-reinforced door. Rose located the right key at once, a heavy eighteenth-century thing that matched the ornate door.

The door yielded, and she peered inside. Her heart beating slightly faster at her own temerity, she found the light switch. The bright neon light flickered on, revealing a large group of statuettes and pottery standing on a long, low table. To one side, a collection of timber packing cases waited to be filled, and there were a few packers' tools—hammers and crowbars—scattered among the ancient artworks.

Rose closed the door behind her, and went over to study the exhibits. It was cold in this underground chamber, but dry and clean. As Andreas Jacobi had said, an ideal place for storing precious old objects.

There were some fine pieces here—a beautiful series of marble portrait busts that matched anything produced in ancient Greece, a vast and wonderful painted urn that was as bright as if it had been done yesterday.

A number of Perspex boxes contained the jewellery

—nothing outstanding by modern standards, but when you considered the limited technology available to the Assyrians a thousand years before Christ, wonderful tributes to human ingenuity and love of beauty. Fascinated, Rose reached out to touch the smooth cold cheeks of the marble portrait busts. So cool, so lovely, their very outlines softened by the immensity of time in which they were conceived. This contribution to the exhibition of Middle Eastern Archaeology was going to be much admired.

A terracotta head caught her eye for an instant. Then she turned away. But her slender brows had come down in a frown. Slowly she turned back. It was a typical piece of Babylonian craftsmanship, the head of a warrior, his ornate beard and helmet painted in much detail with blue spirals, now faded against the rose-pink clay.

Yet there was something wrong with the outline.

Rose's experienced eyes detected something faulty in those flowing lines. She couldn't say exactly what. Yet the more she stared at the larger-than-life piece of sculpture, the more uneasy she became. She leaned forward, peering at the smooth surface. A cold shock jolted her stomach.

The head was unquestionably a fake.

But it couldn't be. It couldn't possibly be a fake. She touched the clay with sensitive fingertips. There was no doubting her instincts—she had just spent three months at Igdir, retrieving pieces exactly like this one from the muddy debris of centuries. And if it hadn't been for that, and the loving lectures which Selman Hristaki had given them all on Babylonian terracotta ware, she might never have spotted the forgery.

She must tell Zoltan at once, warn him that somehow a fake had crept into the collection——

She stopped, feeling cold again. She recalled that

heavy book that Zoltan had written, the book he had shown her that first day in this very house. It had been called *The Babylonians.*

It was impossible that an expert on Babylonian archaeology could have been fooled by this piece.

In her heart, she knew that Zoltan Stendhal must be fully aware that this head was a forgery.

Was this why he had been so violently opposed to letting his guests see the exhibits? Because he knew that Rose would be likely to spot the fake head?

'Oh, God,' she whispered to herself, her voice dry in the cold of the cellar. 'What's this all about, Zoltan?'

She picked the head up carefully. It was very good, an excellent piece of artistic and archaeological fraud. It had obviously fooled Andreas Jacobi, just as it was going to fool experts on the other side of the Atlantic.

But why? What conceivable reason could Zoltan have for sending a fake exhibit to a prestigious international exhibition? As some kind of dry joke?

Rose held the heavy thing in both hands, staring at the blue-painted eyes, the fierce snarl that so convincingly twisted the warrior's lips—and prayed that this was a joke, and nothing more. Suddenly a spasm of fear shook her. If Zoltan found her here, examining the forgery, he would certainly be furious. Hastily she tried to replace the warrior's head on its stand. But her trembling fingers were clumsy, and the smooth clay slipped slightly.

She bit her lip fiercely as the delicate pottery cracked against the edge of the table. Cursing under her breath, she hefted the head upwards to examine the damage.

'Oh, damn!'

There was a distinct crack running in a wide circle around the corner of the neck. It was on the bottom, though, and with luck—with a lot of luck—it might never be spotted.

Yet there was something else wrong. This head shouldn't have been sealed off at the neck, as though it were a container of some kind. It should have been open at the bottom——

A container.

Holding the head against her chest, Rose prised at the crack feverishly with her fingernails. With a little snap, a circular chunk of terracotta came away, leaving a dark hole into the interior of the head.

Laying the piece down with trembling fingers, she lifted the head to peer inside it. There was something inside, something that had been packed tightly into the interior of the forged head. Her questing fingers felt smooth plastic.

Frantically, she tugged hard, and drew out a little plastic packet. It was filled with a fine white powder.

Stunned, she dropped it, and dug her fingers inside. There were more. At least a dozen little plastic packets, filled with an innocent-looking white powder.

Except that this powder was as innocent as poison. The most horrible poison ever devised to bring deadly dreams to human minds craving for escape.

Her hands flew to her pale cheeks, her eyes wide.

'Oh no,' she whispered. 'Oh, Zoltan, *no!*'

CHAPTER SEVEN

SHE sat there, stunned into incomprehension. In her horror, one strange thought kept on re-echoing through her mind.

How swiftly Sarai's Tarot reading had come true.

She stared blindly at the little white packages, strewn along the table among the vases and marble busts under the pitiless neon light. A pain more cruel and savage than anything she had felt before had taken hold of her heart and mind. The very depth of her love for Zoltan was driving the dagger deeper into her soul, bringing the wonderful castles of her dreams tumbling silently down around her.

She wiped the tears absently from her cheeks, no longer able to cry. She was remembering something Freddie had said as a young doctor, after returning from a day working with drug addicts in London.

'The people who peddle this filth are the worst criminals on the face of this planet,' he had said bitterly. 'Worse than murderers. They're responsible for the death and torture of thousands of innocent young lives . . .'

God, how trusting she had been, how naïve! She had been so prepared to take Zoltan at face value, blinded by that magnificent face and physique, fooled by that brilliant mind. Now she was having to reconsider everything she knew about him.

Everything? Bitterly, she realised that she knew next to nothing about him. What *had* he been doing up in the hills of Agri that snowy morning? She had swallowed the tale about the bandits so readily. Now . . .

And the fierce pain of that blow. The ease with

which he had knocked down a helpless human being. The ruthless power which lay just beneath the urbane manner and the soft, deep voice.

And where *did* Zoltan get his money from? On the stock exchange? That was another glib tale she had been eager to swallow. Painfully, she was having to accept that these deadly little packets of powder might provide the answer to all her questions. An unbearable answer. An answer that was going to mean the end of all her happiness for ever.

Slowly her feelings cooled, steadied. This was something too important to be left in doubt. There was still a chance, no matter how faint, that there was an innocent answer to these white packages. She had to know. Quickly she unfolded one of the packets. The powder inside had no smell, and she was too frightened to taste it. She spread a tissue on the ground, and shook half a teaspoon of the powder into it. Then she sealed the plastic packet again and twisted her sample up, dropping the tissue package into her bag.

Carefully, working with desperate calm, she replaced the packages inside the hollow head, stuffing them inside as securely as she could.

Now, how to seal the head up again? There was a little bottle of clear nail varnish in her bag. She painted the jagged edges of the piece she had broken, and pressed it back into place. Waiting for it to dry, she listened for any sound of Zoltan returning.

Oh, dear God, let it be all right, she prayed. Let this be a joke of some kind, a crazy joke—anything except what it looks like!

The nail varnish was holding the cracked piece securely now. But the circular crack was still visible. Rose looked around hastily. There was a sprinkling of dust behind the exhibits. Wetting her finger, she wiped the dust into a thin smear and rubbed it carefully into the crack.

After a few applications, the crack was all but invisible. Unless you were looking for it, it couldn't be seen. Her heart pounding, she placed the head back on its stand, and looked around. She hadn't disturbed anything she could see. A little jolt of panic made her run to the door. If Zoltan found her here——

She switched the light off, and locked the door with shaking fingers. Not a mouse was stirring in the house. She tiptoed silently back up the stairs, along the corridor, and into the drawing-room.

The night had settled in while she had been underground, and it was dark. Only the red glow of the fire lit the big room. She slid the keys back on to the coffee-table, getting them into as close to their original position as she could, and then stood in front of the fire, pressing her hands to her aching, thudding heart.

The sample was secure in her bag. She would get it to a chemist as soon as possible, and ask for an analysis. And when the answer came—she shut her mind to the thought of what she would do if the powder did turn out to be some kind of drug. She would let tomorrow take care of itself.

Slowly she sank into a chair, trying to still the pounding of her heart. If only there were some drink she could take that would silence the memory, erase it! If only she could go back and cancel that horrific act of discovery in the cellar. But she couldn't.

She lay back, closing her eyes, her long chestnut hair spread out over the cushion, and let out a long, shuddering sigh. Who was there to turn to? Only Sarai Murat, or Andy Jacobi. Tonight, she decided firmly, she was going to phone Freddie in Chicago, and tell him everything. He would advise her, tell her what to do——

Her eyes flicked open as she heard the sound of Zoltan's returning car. At all costs he must not know that she had discovered his secret. For all she knew, others of those objects might also be fakes, stuffed with that bland white powder. She sat up, shaking a little, listening to the sounds of the car door slamming, and the courtyard door opening.

'Rose?'

'Oh, Zoltan,' she said, her voice almost a sob.

'What is it, beloved?' His voice was deep with concern. 'Why are you sitting in the dark?'

'Don't put the light on,' she pleaded. She didn't want him to see her eyes, and perhaps read the truth there. In the fireglow, she saw his tall figure move over to her. He sat down beside her, his arms reaching for her. Forgetting everything in the warmth of his presence, Rose nestled against his broad chest, revelling in the musky man-smell of his body.

'You're still trembling,' he said thoughtfully. 'I think you're sickening for something, hmm? Maybe a touch of 'flu.'

'It'll pass,' she murmured.

'Tonight you'll go to bed with a hot whisky and two Paracetamol,' he commanded. 'I think you should spend the night here.'

'Oh, no,' she said urgently. 'I'll be fine, Zoltan—I promise.'

'But you're not well,' he said quietly, his breath warm against her neck. 'I'm worried about you.'

'It's nothing,' she repeated. Her eyes had grown accustomed to the dim firelight, and she stared up wonderingly into his beautiful face. Could this man really be a drug smuggler, a callous destroyer of human life and happiness? 'I often get this,' she went on, improvising. 'It's a feminine weakness . . .'

'Oh,' he said with a smile. 'Are you sure that's all it is?'

'Believe me.'

'I'd believe you if you told me the moon was made

of Cheddar,' he said, tracing the smooth outline of her cheek with his fingers. 'Listen, darling, I'm sorry I snapped at you about those exhibits earlier on.'

'I didn't notice,' she put in nervously.

'I didn't meant to hurt you. But I have my reasons for wanting those things to stay safe. Do you forgive me?'

'You know I do,' she whispered—and thought, with a pang of guilt, of the little twist of tissue paper in her handbag. Zoltan ran his fingers gently through her hair, and her eyes fluttered closed under the sensual caress.

'What was Andy saying to you on the balcony this afternoon?'

'Nothing,' she sighed. 'Just about the trees and the time of year.'

'You looked so very serious about it. And I noticed you were shaking then.'

'I—I've been a bit shaky all day,' she said, confused. 'Maybe it's you that does it to me.'

'Maybe,' he said, the smile deep in his voice. 'Shall I tell you what you do to me?'

'Zoltan——'

'Rose, there's so much I want to say to you, so much I want to show you.' She clung to his strong arms, melting to the warmth in his voice, in his closeness to her. 'You don't know just how much I want you . . .'

The roughness in his normally velvet-smooth voice made her breathing quicken. Her fingers stirred against his arms.

'But how long will you want me for?' she asked, searching for the truth in those dark eyes. 'My mind's a whirl, Zoltan . . .'

'Yes. Things have happened so fast, so very fast. Would you ever have dreamed, that day in the cave, that you and I would come to this?' He touched her lips with his fingers. 'This is like being on a roller-coaster, isn't it? It's almost too fast, too delicious. Sometimes I think you're too good to be true, Rose.'

'Me?' She could scarcely believe him. Could a man like this really feel that kind of passion for her? Was the implication in his words really truthful? If Zoltan felt more than simple desire for her, if his feeling went beyond sex into the depth of true emotion, then she was caught up in something that was almost frighteningly powerful.

This was no college infatuation, as her relationship with Barry had been. Nor was Zoltan the self-loving weakling that Barry had been. He was a man, with a man's formidable passions and emotions. Once the train of his love had been set in motion, there would be no stopping it. And for her, caught up in that burning passion, there could be no middle way. It would be either make or break.

'I hate to see you looking so unhappy,' he said gently. 'Can't I get you something—a painkiller?'

'No, thank you.' It would take more than medicine to kill this pain. 'Just hold me.'

'There's nothing I'd rather do,' he smiled, taking her to him. Rose nestled against him. He smelt of man, musky and exciting, and of some aromatic aftershave. Dreamily, she looked up into his face above her.

'I need you, Rose,' he whispered. The firelight had put a tiny flame in each eye as he looked down at her. 'I need you. I've never said that to another human being before.'

Can I believe you? she wanted to cry. Or do you say that to all the women who lie in your arms, loving you and trusting you, and being betrayed by you?

'Zoltan,' she said shakily, 'I—I'm out of my depth with all this. All these—these feelings. They're very new to me. Don't be impatient with me . . .'

'Not impatient *with* you, darling,' he said in a voice

like warm velvet. 'Impatient *for* you. Impatient to possess your heart, Rose. Impatient to make your soul quicken with mine.'

His kiss was hot against her forehead, and then she felt his lips brush each of her eyelids, sealing them into a languorous trance.

'Please tell me—have you ever felt like this with another woman?' She raised her heavy lids to look into those splendid eyes. 'Have you ever said these things before?'

'What makes you ask that?' he enquired, stroking her full lips with his fingers. 'Can't you read the answer in your own heart? This only happens between a man and a woman once in their lifetimes, Rose.'

'Promise,' she pleaded.

'Why so unsure, sweet Rose? I promise.'

Easily given. Promises as sweet and as cheap as candy to silence a complaining child frightened of the dark.

'You frighten me, Zoltan Stendhal,' she whispered.

'It is love that frightens you,' he smiled. 'As it frightens me.' He gathered her in his arms, his mouth claiming hers with a slow passion that burned through her like a grass fire, spreading steadily to every area of her mind and heart.

Shutting her mind to all the devils of doubt that were screaming at her, Rose strained against him, accepting his kiss with an answering passion, intoxicated by the warmth of his mouth and the strength in his arms, her breasts crushed against his chest. She wanted him to overwhelm her, a tidal wave to drown all her anxieties, all the nagging fears and doubts in her.

Hungrily, scarcely knowing what she was doing, she inhaled the air from his lungs into her own, furnace-hot and as giddy-making as strong wine, as though she could drink his very man's spirit, make him a part of her that would never be let go. They clung to one another in the fire's gentle glow, the dark room silent but for the crackling of the logs; and then, slowly, their mouths still locked in a kiss, Zoltan pulled her body off the chair and on to the thick Persian rug on the floor. Without thinking, she moved her hands under the clinging silk of his sweater and slid her palms hungrily across the velvet skin that covered the hard muscles of his back. She wanted to touch every inch of him, to caress every tense, taut sinew in his body, to make him hers for ever.

And his own fingers were tugging roughly at the buttons of her blouse, making her gasp as his hand slid across the silk of her ribs. A surge of emotion made her twist in his arms as he unhooked her bra, his hand caressing back across her side to cup her full breast possessively. His thumb brushed across her nipple, and she arched her back, her mouth clinging to his as she pulled away.

Her heart was bursting with words of love, with the mad, wonderful things she wanted to say to him; that she adored him, worshipped him, feared him. That she begged him to be patient and gentle with her. That she trusted him, no matter what . . .

Now his kisses had become gentle, butterfly wings that brushed her temples and cheeks, that whispered maddeningly sweet things in her ears, that drifted down her neck and paused in the hollow of her throat, tasting the warm scent there, swelling on her racing pulse. And her own fingers, clinging to him, could feel his heart beating in time with hers, a rough, wild rhythm that was driving him fiercely onwards.

'Rose, sweet Rose,' he whispered, his voice husky, 'I want you so much! Your mouth is as soft as a dove's breast, your hair smells of summer . . . If only you knew how you've haunted me these past weeks!' He pressed his face against the soft, scented warmth of her breasts, his fingers biting into her shoulders hard enough to hurt. 'I can't think of anything else except you. Nothing matters to me any more. Tell me you feel the same.'

'Zoltan——' she gasped.

'Tell me!' he commanded. 'Tell me what you feel, for God's sake! Don't torment me like this . . .'

Dimly, through the haze of her ecstasy, she became aware that he was begging *her* for comfort, that he needed her, wanted her! Her laugh of joy was almost a sob.

'Darling, don't you know?' she whispered. 'Don't you know how I feel?'

His mouth found the tender peak of her breast, guiding it into an aching star of passion, making her shudder in his embrace.

'You're so lovely,' he whispered against her skin. 'You're my doe, Rose, my sweet white doe . . .'

'And you,' she whispered back, 'my hunter, my lord . . .' Their kiss was deep, sweet, an ocean of union and shared love.

And slowly, unbidden, like the grey blur of a shark in dark water, came the memory. The memory of a snarling warrior's head. A head filled with little packages of death, the white powder of poisonous dreams.

Shuddering, she drew away from him, her lips now cold against his.

'What is it?' he murmured, caressing her glossy hair.

'I—I feel ill,' she whimpered. 'Oh, Zoltan, my love—I'm so sorry. Please—take me home.'

'Spend the night here,' he said urgently, sitting up to look into her pale face. 'I'll have a bed made up for you, get a doctor over——'

'There's no need for a doctor,' she replied, forcing a smile. 'I'll be fine in the morning.'

'My poor Rose!' He cradled her in his arms. Hating

herself for deceiving him, hating what she had to do, Rose bit back the tears of frustration and pain.

'I'm sorry for doing this to you,' she whispered. And prayed that he would remember that apology in the future, if the worst came to the worst. Remember it, and understand.

'It's you I feel sorry for,' he smiled. Slowly he rose to his feet, and helped her up. 'Are your legs as wobbly as mine?' he asked wryly. 'You make me weak, Rose.'

'What do you know of weakness, you who are so strong?' She picked up her handbag. As though the twist of paper inside it were a block of radium, she felt its guilty heat in her fingers. 'I'm sorry, Zoltan.'

'Hush,' he said, kissing her firmly on the lips. 'I'll drive you home right away.'

Holding her close against his side, he led her out into the night.

Rose sat tense and silent in the car, and after she had said goodbye to Zoltan in the foyer of her hotel, she locked herself in her room and threw herself on the bed.

Misery washed over her. She hated betraying Zoltan, no matter what he was. More, she hated the idea that Zoltan could be even remotely associated with any kind of illegal activity.

She checked her wristwatch. It was six in the evening here. What did that mean—early morning in Chicago?

Impulsively she picked up the bedside telephone, and asked the operator to put a call through to Freddie's number in Chicago. Within a minute she heard her brother's sleepy voice echoing distantly down the line.

'Freddie! It's me!'

'Rosie?' She heard a muffled yawn. 'Where are you calling from?'

'Istanbul, Turkey. How are you?'

'Me? I'm fine. Fine.' Another muffled yawn, and then Freddie's voice livened up. 'Hey, it's great to hear from you! How was the dig at whatsisname?'

'Igdir. It was fine. It's good to hear you, Freddie!' There was a wide grin across her face. It was wonderful to hear Freddie's voice again, despite the overtones of an American accent he had picked up during three years in Chicago.

'Great to hear from you, Rosie. Listen, how about coming to Chicago for a month or two? I've got some leave coming up—and I'll pay your air fare. We'll see a bit of the country. What say? Interested?'

'Of course I'm interested,' Rose laughed, sitting down on her bed with pink cheeks. 'But I'm rather tied up just now, Freddie——'

'A man?'

'Something like that,' she acknowledged.

'You like him?'

'I love him.' The words simply came out, as naturally as that. She heard Freddie's slow chuckle.

'Terrific! What's his name? Who is he?'

'I'll tell you all that in a letter,' she promised. 'Right now, big brother, I need your advice.'

'Is that why you're calling me at this ungodly hour of the morning?' he sighed. 'What is it? Nothing to do with having a baby, is it?'

'You know me better than that,' she said in mock-horror. Her face went a little grimmer. 'It's serious, Freddie. I don't know quite what to do.'

'Spill the beans,' Freddie advised. 'This call will cost you a fortune if you don't make it snappy.'

'It's about a friend—a good friend. I've got evidence that he may—just may—be involved in drug dealing——'

'Evidence?' Her brother's query cut sharply into her sentence. 'What kind of evidence, Rose?'

'I found some plastic bags of white powder in—in his suitcase,' she improvised. 'I don't know, but it looks to me like chalk dust. Is that likely to be any drug you know?'

'Heroin,' Freddie said succinctly. 'Listen to me, Rose. Where are you calling from?'

'My hotel—the Divan, in Taxim Square.'

'Got that. Is this so-called friend of yours anywhere in the vicinity?'

'No, but——'

'No buts, Rose. Now do exactly as I say. You get over to the nearest police station right away. Don't talk to anyone on the way, don't tell anyone where you're going. Just get over there, and tell the local police chief exactly what you know.'

'But Freddie——'

'And then you *stay* there. Got that? You tell them to keep you there until they've got this guy under wraps.'

'But Freddie, I can't!'

'Rose, for God's sake! Guys who deal in hard drugs like heroin don't play for peanuts! Do you have any idea what they'll do to you if they get any inkling that you've found their stuff?'

An icy chill rolled down Rose's spine.

'But I'm not sure that this white powder really *is* anything serious.'

'Are you crazy? Guys don't keep talcum powder in plastic bags hidden in their suitcases. But that's exactly the way they keep heroin. Or morphine, or cocaine. It's all poison, Rose. And it's all worth its weight in diamonds. You're talking about millions of dollars, Rose, and some very heavy people. Now for Pete's sake, do as I say—get yourself into the local cop-shop, and stay there!'

'Freddie, I'm not in any danger.'

'How do you know that?'

'I just do. I took a little sample of this powder stuff——'

'You did *what*?'

'—and I was thinking of asking a chemist to do an analysis on it. Then I'd know for sure.'

'Rosie, Rosie,' she heard her brother groan, 'you're as mad as twenty hatters! You'll end up in a Turkish jail, girl—and believe me, they're the worst! And they hate drug offenders——'

'What else can I do?' she pleaded.

'How much of this stuff have you got?' he demanded.

'I don't know. About half a teaspoonful.'

'And you say it's a pure white powder?'

'Just like chalk dust,' she nodded.

'You don't need a chemist, Rose. Just mix it with water. If it dissolves into a colourless liquid, then it's heroin. If it floats on the surface, you've got talcum-powder. Can you do that?'

'Yes,' she nodded, her heart thudding painfully. 'Hold on, Freddie.' Tucking the receiver under her arm, she reached over to the basin, and filled a tooth-glass with half an inch of water. Then she knelt on the floor, took the twist of tissue-paper out of her bag, and tipped it with shaking fingers into the water.

The powder swirled, dissolved, disappeared.

She stared at the innocent-looking liquid, ready to cry. Just a few drops of water. Enough to wash away a whole life's happiness.

Numbly she put the receiver to her ear.

'It dissolved,' she said, her voice almost inaudible.

'Heroin,' Freddie said grimly. 'I told you so. What else could it be? Now, throw that water out, Rose. It's deadly. Wash the glass thoroughly, and wash your hands with soap and water. Whatever you carried your sample in, flush it down the toilet. Got that?'

'Yes,' she whispered.

'And as soon as you ring off, Rose, get straight on to the police.'

'Oh, Freddie!'

'This drug-smuggler of yours—he doesn't happen to be the guy you're in love with, does he?'

'Yes,' she confessed miserably. A word she had never heard her normally patient brother use before came drifting distinctly down the line.

'That's very tough, little sister. But you're going to have to go through with this. Otherwise you'll end up floating down the Bosphorus. And a lot of kids somewhere are going to die a very nasty death.'

She closed her eyes in pain, her heart ready to break.

'Are you listening to me, Rose?'

'Yes,' she gritted.

'Now do as I say. Clear everything away, call the cops, and for God's sake don't mention anything about having taken a sample, or you'll end up in the hoosegow with your friend. I'm going to ring off now, Rose. I'll call you back in twenty minutes—and I want to hear that you've gone to the police.' She sat in silent misery. 'Otherwise I'll get the National Guard out, Rosie. I mean it.'

'Okay,' she whispered. 'I'll do what you say.'

'Right. Sweetie, I'm so very sorry,' he said more gently. 'I realise this must be hell for you—but lives are at stake here. Smuggling heroin is worse than murder—much worse.'

'I know,' she breathed.

'I'll call back in twenty minutes. I love you, little sister.'

'Love you, Freddie.' Brokenly, Rose replaced the receiver and bowed her head on to her knees, too sad even to cry. Zoltan, my Zoltan! My beautiful dark huntsman, my love—lost for ever . . .

Slowly she lay on her side, curling up like a child in pain. The telephone waited, its old-fashioned face accusing. She shut her eyes, and let her thoughts wander back to that blissful night on the Black Sea. The happiest night of her life. How deliciously cool the water had been, how strong Zoltan's arms.

She was still lost in her reverie when the telephone shrilled. She sat up with a start, her heart beating. God! She hadn't called the police yet—and Freddie had promised to do so if she hadn't done it by the time he phoned.

She snatched the receiver up.

'Freddie?'

'Have you called the police yet?'

She opened her mouth, her mind racing. Zoltan's face swam into her mind, and she squeezed her eyes shut.

'Yes,' she said firmly. 'Yes, I've called them. They're coming round to pick me up in a few minutes. And they're going to arrest my—my—friend.'

'Thank heaven for that!' Freddie breathed. 'Good girl. I can imagine how it must have hurt—but you did the right thing. Listen, call me tomorrow morning, first thing. Okay?'

'Okay,' she said lifelessly.

'I'm going to get on to Nathaniel Evans in London—the family lawyer. He'll contact you as soon as possible. What police station will you be at?'

'Oh—er—Istanbul Central,' she stammered.

'Good. I'll speak to you again in the morning. Look after yourself, Rosie.'

'You too.'

And she laid the receiver slowly back on its cradle. She had lied to Freddie. Strangely, she felt no guilt. There was something she owed Zoltan—a period of mourning, almost. She lay back on the bed, cradling her head in her arms. She would call the police tomorrow. She couldn't do it now. She simply couldn't . . .

CHAPTER EIGHT

ROSE awoke from turbulent dreams with a gasp of fear. Zoltan was leaning over her, brushing the silky hair back from her cheeks.

'It's only me,' he smiled. 'You should lock your door in strange hotels.'

'Wh-what are you doing here?' she stammered, trying to sit upright.

'I knocked, but you didn't hear.' He leaned forward and kissed her firmly, full on the lips. 'Welcome to the land of the living, sweetheart. I came by to see how you were this morning.'

She blinked around. It was broad daylight, and the distant sounds of busy Istanbul were filtering through her window with the autumn sunlight.

'I'm fine,' she nodded, gathering her hair back. The horrible events of the night before came rolling back, and she looked at Zoltan with wide brown eyes. Did he know that she had found the heroin? He was heart-stoppingly handsome in a conservative charcoal suit, his red tie matching a rose in his lapel. His piercing grey eyes studied her.

'Yes, you look better. I thought these might cheer you up.' She looked at the huge spray of roses—red as the one in his lapel—in the vase beside her bed. Her love for him came welling up at the kind gesture.

'Thank you, Zoltan.' She sat up in the bed, fear still nagging at her. Had he found out? She didn't think so. The smile that curled on that stunning mouth was warm, sexy. 'I'm sorry I was such a drip last night,' she said awkwardly.

'You were ill,' he shrugged. His eyes dropped with

flattering interest to her breasts. 'How beautiful you are when you sleep, Rose.'

'Am I?' Aware that the shadows of her nipples were quite visible through the thin negligee, she drew the blankets chastely up over her chest. Zoltan's smile was mocking.

'Why cover such beauty? You're like the sea anemones I used to play with on the beaches when I was a boy. When they think they're unnoticed, they blossom into beautiful flowers. But at the first touch, they shrink back into themselves in panic.' He picked up one of her hands, studying the slender fingers. 'You sleep like a little girl, innocent and open-mouthed. That doesn't stop me wanting you.'

'Oh,' Rose said nervously. His fingers locked through hers again, that caress that was so strangely intimate and touching.

'What shall we do today?' he asked, his bronzed face full of happiness. 'If you're feeling well enough, that is. A picnic on the Aegean? Or would you rather see the forests of Zonguldak?'

'Zoltan——'

'Rose of the morning,' he said, bowing over her hand with mock-deference, 'thy wish is my command. Command thy slave but to fetch the silver moon, or the apples of the sun.'

'You'd never be any woman's slave,' she said wryly, looking at him with an aching heart.

'True,' he smiled, the tiger-light back in his eyes. 'I am more accustomed to command than to obey. Yet there is one part of me that lacks a mistress.'

'Which part?' she wanted to know, falling in with the dangerous, delicious game of his flirtation.

'My heart, of course.' His caress was light against her cheek, yet it seemed to leave her whole body tingling. She flinched away from his touch, confusion reigning in her mind.

'Why do you wince? I'd never hurt you, Rose.'

'Never?' Her eyes were dark as she stared into his face, the face she would never forget. 'Not even if I did something terrible to you?'

'I find it hard to imagine you doing anything remotely terrible,' he laughed. With irresistible arms, he drew her forward, kissing her eyelids with warm lips. 'What can the matter be, Rose of my heart? Have you dreamed of something that frightened you?'

'Yes,' she whispered. 'I had horrible dreams, Zoltan.'

'You're still a child sometimes,' he smiled, caressing the silky head that was laid against his shoulder. 'I think you need a man in your bed.'

'No!' she said nervously, her stomach jolting at the thought that he might climb into her bed with her. He threw his head back to laugh.

'I mean when you sleep,' he purred. 'Someone to chase the shadows away.'

'I'm quite capable of looking after myself,' she said stiffly. She was on edge this morning, unable to deal with the erotic challenge that Zoltan always presented.

'You're so tense,' he murmured. 'What is it, *chérie*? Are you afraid of me?'

'No,' she whispered.

He held her close, his mouth brushing hers in a long, warm caress.

'What is it, then? Are you tired of this game?'

'I don't——' She was silenced by his lips.

Zoltan had kissed her before, kisses that set her heart alight, and made the blood pound in her ears; but this time was different. This time he transcended everything else. His need for her reached through everything that stood between them, touching the innermost part of her soul.

She sank against him, her eyes shutting out the world around her. He kissed her exquisitely slowly, his lips unhurried, his fingers lost in the curls of her hair. As though she were drifting away from her own body, she hung on his neck to keep her hold on reality; and when at last he drew back to smile down at her with deep, diamond-bright eyes, she felt shaken, her breath barely stirring in her lungs.

'Something is wrong, *ma petite*,' he said quietly, tracing the beautiful curve of her cheekbone with one finger. 'Something is troubling you. I can feel it in your kiss. I can see it in your enchanting eyes.'

'No—nothing,' she whispered.

'You're hiding something,' he said silkily. 'Perhaps your mouth will tell me in its own way.'

And he kissed her again with sensual force teasing her lips into a response. Scarcely knowing what she was doing, Rose dug her nails into his back, arching up to meet his body with taut passion.

And in that moment she knew that she loved this man, loved him as she would never love again. The agony of having to betray him tore at her heart. How could she? What woman could sentence the man she loved to imprisonment, perhaps even death?

She was white and tight-lipped as he released her. Zoltan's dark brows came down, his fingers biting into her arms.

'For God's sake, what is it, Rose? Are you hurting inside? Tell me!'

'I can't,' she cried out, covering her face. 'Zoltan, please leave me. I beg you.'

'What is it? Is it another man?'

'Oh, no,' she whispered, finding the courage to smile at him. 'Nothing like that.'

'You're not already married, are you?' he demanded, his face tense, his own mouth taut with worry.

'I swear it, nothing like that. Just let me be for a few hours, Zoltan. I must be alone. I must!'

He stared into her face for long seconds. When he spoke, his voice was harsh.

'I don't like what's happening, Rose. You've been acting strangely for the past twenty-four hours now.'

'It's my own business,' she told him. 'I have to work this out in my own way.'

'Won't you let me help you?' he asked quietly. 'I'm more understanding than you seem to imagine.'

'There's nothing you can do.' Afraid that she was going to cry, and spill out her secret, Rose twisted away from him. 'Zoltan, for God's sake, go!'

'If you wish it so much,' he said in a dry voice. He took a gold pen and a card from his pocket and scribbled down a number. 'That's my home number, Rose. I'm going to be there all day. Will you promise to call me if you need me?'

She took the slip of paper, nodding.

'I promise.'

'I'm coming to see you again tonight.' He held up a hand to silence her protests. 'Whether you like it or not. You mean too much to me, Rose. And if you're feeling better tonight, my sweet one, I may just tell you exactly how much you mean to me.'

She stared at him with dark eyes. Somehow she sensed that he was utterly sincere. No matter what he had done, no matter what he was, she knew that Zoltan Stendhal's feeling for her was true.

And that nearly broke her heart there and then.

'What can you possibly see in me?' she asked, almost to herself. 'You could have any woman you wanted, you know that . . .'

'Can I?' He smiled wryly. 'It seems to me that I can't have the one woman I do want. What do I see in you? Beauty. It's as simple as that, my dear. You have a very rare quality, Rose; the quality of being beautiful. It draws people to you like a magnet.'

'But I'm such a country mouse——'

'You're as gentle and as beautiful as a Madonna,' he said quietly. 'There's a light in your eyes, a kind of luminous quality to your whole being. It's unmistakable. It picks you out from a million others, and draws me to you. It tells me that you're good, that you have that rare purity, that inward beauty——' He shook his head. 'I can't put it into words, Rose. If I could, maybe it wouldn't mean as much as it does.' He touched her cheek almost reverently. 'There are some men who could express it in a poem, or a painting, or some unimaginably sweet music. But I don't envy them. In a way, not being able to explain you, not being able to explain what you do to me—well, that sort of keeps it inside me for ever. Locks it away in my heart.'

Rose shuddered, her mind floating drowsily on the bittersweet litany of his words, her heart tasting their truth, their secret meaning, only for her.

'I can only show you what I mean,' he said, his voice like satin against her ultra-sensitive flesh. 'I can only ask you to give me the time, the oceans of time, that I need to show you what I really feel about you.'

'Ask?' She smiled languorously, her soul stirred like sea-water before a storm. 'That doesn't suit you, my love. You were born to command.'

'And yet I do not command you,' he smiled. 'Not yet. A good horseman recognises a truly fine spirit, just as a great swordsman recognises a worthy adversary. You are not to be bullied and commanded, my Rose. If I'm to have you, then I shall have to coax you, tempt you——' His kiss clung to her lips like heady wine. '—bribe you with kisses and honey. But you will be mine. I promise you that.'

'Zoltan——'

'Your face has haunted me, Rose, ever since that strange day in the cave. When I saw you lying there, your amber eyes dark with pain, your hair tumbling loose against the snow, my heart stopped inside me. Can you imagine my remorse? And then, weeks later, to find you tiptoeing along my corridors——' He grinned. '*La forza del destino*, Rose. It was Fate. What else?' He looked at her drooping mouth, her weary eyes. 'I've tired you out. You're still not well. I'll leave you, Rose, and get back to the Street of the Fountain. Just promise me you'll tell me what all this melancholy was about one day. Yes?'

'I promise,' she sighed, still burning with his words. 'I promise.'

He rose with a slight sigh. 'It goes against my heart to leave you while you're like this. Look after yourself, *ma chérie*.' The desire and the tenderness in his eyes twisted a dagger in her heart. Feeling like Judas, Rose accepted the kiss he gave her, and watched him walk to the door.

'By the way,' he smiled, turning back to look at her, 'I wanted to tell you that I've just finished *The Etruscan Darkness*. Andreas gave me some help with the proof-reading, so I finished earlier than I anticipated.'

'Oh, Zoltan, I'm so glad for you!' Why, she wondered desperately, why would a man with so much talent, so much to give the world, defile himself with drug trafficking? 'I know it's going to be a worldwide success. It deserves to be.'

'Thanks.' He raised his hand in a semi-ironic salute. 'Don't forget what I've said, Rose. Look after yourself.'

As the door closed behind him, she had to bite her knuckles to keep back the tears that were waiting.

She lay back on the bed, unable to move for the pain in her heart, a physical pain that shook her and wrung her nerves like a fever. She closed her eyes, and lay still for what seemed like an eternity, waiting for the grief to subside. She refused to allow herself the luxury of tears. She felt she didn't deserve it. There would be time for tears later. Half an hour drifted by.

Then, as if in a daze, she clambered out of bed, washed, and started dressing. If she was ever going to do it, she realised, then she must do it now, at once. Because the longer she left it, the more impossible it would become. She pulled a fawn slacks suit over a white cotton T-shirt, and slipped her supple boots on. Picking up her comb, she went to the mirror and tried to restore some order to her sleep-tumbled hair.

The face that looked back at her was pale, more than ever like a Florentine Madonna. She wasn't surprised to see the smudges of weariness under her eyes, or the slant of bitterness to her full mouth. She turned away, unable to meet her own accusing eyes, and ordered coffee from the room service.

Drinking it half an hour later, she began screwing up her courage. Zoltan would be at home now. He had told her so. Playing himself unknowingly into her trap.

She reached for the telephone, then froze, her hand on the receiver. Her heart almost failed her.

It was the thought of the destruction and suffering that those drugs would bring to thousands of innocent young people that finally decided her. Blotting out the picture of Zoltan's face, she remembered the slouching, painfully thin figures she had seen in the streets of Soho, minds and bodies ravaged by their addiction. With clenched teeth she jerked up the receiver and asked the receptionist to connect her with the central police station in the city.

There was a slight delay as they searched for someone who spoke English. Then a businesslike male voice came on the line.

'Inspector Yasir Kasim here. Who is calling, please?'

'I've got some very important information,' she said breathlessly.

'Yes? What information?'

'About a consignment of drugs that is about to be

shipped to America. Hidden in some archaeological exhibits.'

'Give me the details,' the voice said sharply.

'The drugs are in a fake Babylonian sculpture,' she said, her eyes shut tight. 'The man behind this is—is—Zoltan Stendhal.'

'Spell that,' he commanded.

She obeyed numbly—and as if in a dream, told him everything.

'And where is this sculpture now?'

'At his house. Number 37, the Street of the Fountain.'

'That's in Sehzdebasi?'

'Yes.'

'Have you any idea how much there is of the drug?'

'I don't know—maybe two pounds.'

'So?' She heard rapid Turkish on the other end, then the Inspector's voice came through again.

'We must speak to you, *madame*. It's vital, if we're to get the charges to stick.'

'Are you—are you sending some men to arrest him.'

'Yes, at once. But we need evidence. Now, what is your name, and where are you?'

'I——' Her voice dried up in her throat. She had done it. She had betrayed Zoltan.

'*Madame*.' The inspector's voice was grim. 'You could be in danger—drug-smugglers are dangerous men.'

'Yes,' she whispered.

'Are you there?' he asked sharply.

'I——'

In a sudden panic, she slammed the receiver down. Oh Zoltan, what are they going to do to you? A horrific image rose up in her mind of Turkish prisons, and all she had heard about them. The Turks hated drug-dealers—Freddie himself had said so.

She couldn't let Zoltan simply be trapped like that.

He was too free, too magnificent ever to go into a cage. Her *beau tigre* of a man—he would be like a lion in shackles.

She snatched up the telephone, her heart trembling.

'Operator? I want to make a private call.'

'The line is free, *madame*.'

Feverishly, Rose dialled the number he had given her. After three subdued burrs, there was a click, and Zoltan's deep voice came on the line.

'Stendhal here.'

'Zoltan, it's me.'

'Rose?' There was concern in his voice. 'What's the matter?'

'There's something I have to tell you,' she said, the words spilling over one another in her haste to get them out. 'The police are coming for you, darling—you must run!'

'What the hell is this all about?' he demanded fiercely.

'When you took Sarai and the others back to town—last night——'

'Yes?'

'I—I took your keys and went down to the cellar. I had a look at the exhibits for New York.' She stopped, panting. His voice was quieter now.

'Go on.'

'I found that head—the Babylonian one. I broke it—by accident——' She closed her eyes at the memory of that moment of horror. 'And I found the drugs inside,' she finished on a whisper. There was a long pause.

'I see,' he said quietly.

'Oh, Zoltan—I've told the police. Please forgive me, my darling—I had to do it! They're coming for you now. For God's sake, try and get away——'

'You've told the police that the drugs are here?' he asked, his voice icy.

'Yes,' she nodded. 'I had to do it.'

There was a long, agonizing silence. Then, she heard him sigh heavily.

'May I ask why you've told me all this?' he asked quietly.

'To give you a chance to escape. I couldn't bear the thought of your suffering, Zoltan. I—I love you.'

'Yet you betrayed me?'

'I couldn't help it,' she cried. 'The thought of what those drugs will do, the young lives it will destroy——'

'Rose,' he said grimly. 'I'm coming over to your hotel right away.'

'No!' she gasped, suddenly terrified of him. She threw the receiver down as though it were a cobra, and snatched up her shoulder-bag. Stuffing a random assortment of clothes inside it, she flung the door open, and ran out into the corridor. She had to get away. But where? Who would shelter her? Now that she'd warned Zoltan that the police were coming, she had cut herself from the law.

As she ran out into the busy street, she remembered. Andy! Gentle Andreas Jacobi, who had warned her against Zoltan in the first place. He would know where she could hide, would know what to do.

There was a phone booth fifty yards up the street, and she walked towards it as fast as she dared. Once inside, she propped her bag on the ledge and hunted frantically through the tattered directory for the University's number.

Please be there, Andy, she implored in her mind, please be there. She dialled the number, dropped in her coin, and asked the receptionist for Andreas Jacobi.

As the gentle voice came on the line, she breathed a sigh of relief.

'Andy? It's Rose Johnson. We met at Zoltan Stendhal's house the other day.'

'Of course. Is anything the matter?'

'Yes,' she said, 'something horrible's happened.' He listened in silence as she spilled out the whole story, down to her last phone call to Zoltan a few minutes ago.

'Can you help me?' she concluded, her knuckles white as she clutched the receiver.

Andy was silent for a short while, then he said slowly,

'This is all—just a bit hard to take in, Rose. Give me a second to assimilate it. You say the police are going to Zoltan's house right now?'

'Yes.'

'And he said he was coming to find you?'

'Yes. What can I do, Andy?'

'You must get out of there, Rose.' The quiet voice was suddenly tense. 'You don't know Zoltan. He's a very dangerous man. If he finds you, he'll kill you for sure!'

She squeezed her eyes shut in horror.

'Rose? Are you still there?'

'Yes.'

'Listen—can you get over here right away? I'll take care of you as best I can—at least until Zoltan's been arrested.'

'Oh, thank you, Andy!' she breathed.

'For God's sake, don't let him see you. Don't tell anyone where you're going. You're in deadly danger, girl.'

'Yes,' she nodded. 'How do I get there?'

'Take the number 42 bus to Bezayit Square. Walk across the square to the University. I'll be waiting for you in front of the fountain. I'm going to get the car ready in the meantime, Rose—I think I'd better take you somewhere safe, somewhere Zoltan doesn't know about. Are you okay?'

'I'm fine,' she said. As fine as a woman can be who's

just betrayed her man. 'I'll be there in half an hour, maybe less. Bless you, Andy.'

'Take care now. And remember, don't tell *anyone* where you're going. I'm no match for Zoltan Stendhal. And I happen to know he's got a gun.'

'Okay,' she nodded, and hung up. She put a hand against the door to push it open—then froze.

A sleek grey sports car pulled to a halt outside her hotel, its tyres screaming, and Zoltan jumped out, his bronzed face grim. Rose cowered back into the booth, but he hadn't seen her. He walked quickly into the hotel, his big frame moving with the speed and grace of some deadly hunting creature. In terror, she slipped out of the phone booth and ran across the traffic to the long line of bus stations at the other end of the square. There was a number 42 just leaving. Fear lending her wings, she ran up to it and sprang on to the steps, clinging to the rail. The driver opened the electric doors, and she scrambled aboard, fighting her way into the crowded interior.

'Bezayit,' she told the conductor, fumbling for coins in her purse—and breathed a prayer of thanks as the bus roared off into the diesel-rich fumes of the Istanbul downtown traffic.

Fear had given way to grief as she walked across the pigeon-thronged square twenty minutes later. She had never felt so empty, so desolate. Inside, she was grieving for what might have been—for a partnership, perhaps even a wonderful marriage—that was now never to be.

And Zoltan—how hard it was to think of that magnificent mind and body as a receptacle for criminal thoughts. It hurt like fury to realise that he was corrupt, that he had turned such power and talent to the service of evil.

It was so—so *mean*, somehow. So mean to use the

horrors of drug addiction simply to make money. She thought of the beautiful houses, the Italian car, the expensive clothes that Zoltan Stendhal obviously enjoyed. All bought, no doubt, with heroin money.

And that day up in the hills—now she knew what he had really been doing up there. He had been collecting the consignment of pure heroin from the Armenian end of the pipeline that stretched from Indo-China in the east to the United States in the west—the secret pipeline that pumped poison into a hundred thousand bloodstreams along the way, bringing crime, torment, and death in its wake.

Her thoughts dark, Rose passed by the ancient second-hand bookstalls in Sahaflar Carsisi, their tables piled high with dilapidated volumes, and through the outer courtyard towards the University.

A slight figure waving caught her attention. It was Andreas Jacobi, wearing the universal khaki jacket and jeans of junior lecturers everywhere. She hurried towards him. The mild face was pale with concern, his weak eyes blinking ten to the dozen.

'Andy, thank God you're here!'

'Did anyone follow you?' he asked anxiously.

'No—but Zoltan arrived at my hotel just as I was coming out of the phone booth——'

Andreas Jacobi's eyes suddenly stopped blinking.

'Did he see you?' he cut through her sentence.

'No—I slipped away, and jumped straight on a bus.'

'You sure he didn't catch a glimpse of you?'

'Sure,' she nodded.

'Fine,' said Andy, his nervous blink returning. He took her arm in a surprisingly strong grasp and hurried her along the the pavement. 'Let's get out of here. I don't fancy encountering Zoltan right now.'

'It's all so terrible,' she said, trying to keep pace with him. 'I just can't believe that he's a drug smuggler. It's all so unreal——'

'I can believe it,' Andy said grimly. 'I told you, didn't I? Zoltan's not what he seems. He's dangerous. Here's the car.'

He unlocked the door of the battered-looking Renault, and Rose climbed inside, clutching her shoulder-bag.

'Where are we going?' she asked him as he got in beside her, and started the engine.

'Somewhere safe,' he said, glancing into the rearview mirror as he eased the little car out into the traffic. She sat in silence as Andy negotiated three sets of traffic-lights, entering a maze of back-streets beside the University.

'God, it's all so awful,' she whimpered, her eyes wet. 'I've never——'

'Did you tell anyone you were coming to meet me?' he interrupted.

'No,' she said numbly. 'There was no one to tell, except—oh, damn!'

'What?'

'Freddie. My brother, Freddie. I told him what had happened last night——'

'Where is he?' Andy cut in.

'In Chicago. I promised to phone him this morning. He'll be worried sick by now.'

'Never mind that,' said Andy, turning right at a crowded intersection. His voice was strange, different somehow. The tentative, mild note in it was gone now.

'But I must phone him, Andy! He'll be crazy with anxiety by now. Can't we stop at a phone booth——'

'There's no time,' Andy said shortly.

'But I must!' She turned to him with worried brown eyes. 'If I don't get through to him——'

'I've said no.'

'Andy, don't be silly——'

'*Will you shut up?*' His voice was shockingly harsh,

and the look he shot her was savage, his small eyes intent. 'Haven't you done enough damage, you little idiot?'

'I—I don't understand,' she stammered, her stomach turning over.

'You don't have to understand,' he said brutally. 'Just sit still and shut up.'

Panic fluttered in her veins. Her mind was still numb from her grief over Zoltan, and she didn't know what was going on—but something was evidently horribly wrong.

A large articulated lorry was in front of them now, and Andreas Jacobi had to slow his car to a snail's pace. He was cursing under his breath, ugly words that made Rose's heart sink even further. Suddenly she knew she had to get out. She fumbled the door-handle open and swung the door out.

'Bitch!' Andy pulled her savagely back into the car, slamming the door and locking it. The car had swerved violently across the road, and there were indignant hoots from behind. 'Try that again and I'll hurt you,' he promised, his voice savage. His left hand on the wheel, he tugged something out of his pocket.

Rose stared with horror at the blue-steel gleam of an automatic pistol in his hand. Holding it crossways across his stomach, Andy pointed the gun at her ribs.

'Andy!' she gasped.

'Shut it. This isn't a toy—and it would give me a great deal of pleasure to shoot you, you interfering little fool!'

'I don't understand,' she gaped, stunned by the reversal of events. 'What—what have I done?'

'You've lost me half a million dollars, for one thing,' he spat out. 'And you've just about got me into a Turkish jail. But you're about to remedy that.' He looked at her, his crooked teeth bared in a mirthless grin. 'You're going to get a chance to put everything right, Rose. Because you're my passport out of this godforsaken country.'

She sat transfixed, gaping at him.

'Now, you've got some questions to answer,' he grated, swinging the wheel one-handed, and letting it go to clash the gears. 'How did you spot that head—the one with the packages inside?'

'I—it was a fake,' she said hoarsely. 'I picked it up and it slipped——'

'You're lying,' he snarled. 'What do you know about Babylonian terracotta?'

'I'm an archaeologist,' she told him. 'I've been working with stuff like that for months.'

'Ah,' he nodded, his fixed grin still in place. 'Zoltan didn't mention that. So that's why he was so reluctant to take you down to see the exhibits that day. What did he say when you told him about the heroin—did he seem surprised?'

'No,' she stammered. 'B-but he must have known that head was a fake.'

'Why?' he snapped. 'It was a superb forgery.'

'It wasn't good enough to fool an expert,' she said.

'You think not? Then you reckon Zoltan knew about it?'

'Of course,' she said. 'But I don't understand——'

'I do. The bastard must have been a police agent.' He banged the wheel with his fist, gnawing at his lower lip. 'God, what a fool I've been! I suspected it, but I should have done something months back.'

'Are you—are you saying that Zoltan didn't put the drugs there?' Rose asked slowly, her mind whirling.

'Zoltan? Of course not.' Andreas Jacobi sneered at her. 'He hasn't got the brains. That was *my* little package you stumbled on, you fool. Half a million dollars' worth of refined heroin. Worth thirty times that on the street.'

'Then it was nothing to do with Zoltan?' she gaped.

'Haven't I just said so?' Andy snarled. 'God, I'd love to see his face when he realises I've got you!'

Rose sat in stunned silence. A surge of joy was rising in her heart. Zoltan had nothing to do with those deadly white packages! The relief seemed to flood her very soul with sunlight, making her want to laugh and cry at the same time. Now she didn't care what happened to her—now that she knew Zoltan was what she had always thought him to be. A faint smile spread across her face, easing away the lines of worry and grief that had settled there over the past few hours.

'You were trying to smuggle that heroin out under cover of the archaeological exhibits,' she said slowly. 'It was all your idea.'

'One of my better ones,' Andy nodded. He had pulled out into the fast lane, and they were now heading through a series of steep cuttings along a motorway. 'It was providential, you telephoning me like that. Otherwise I'd have ended up in the hot seat—with my partners.'

'Why did you tell me to beware of Zoltan—that he wasn't what he seemed?' she asked.

'Because I hate him,' said Andreas Jacobi, his thin face distorted into a snarl. 'I've always hated those sort of people—big, self-confident, handsome bastards, always getting their own way with women and money!'

In fascinated horror, Rose watched his face, for the first time seeing into the soul of this little, embittered man.

'No one notices me,' he was saying venomously. 'No one's noticed me since I was a child. They don't even look into my eyes. They're too busy looking at the show-offs and the loudmouths, the people who blow their own trumpets.'

'I don't think it's like that,' she murmured. But knew it to be the truth—no one would ever have bothered to look closely at Andreas Jacobi, a mild, blinking man with a heart bursting with hatred against his fellow humans. As if reading her thoughts, Andy nodded.

'Yeah, I'm the original invisible man. Well, I learned to make that work for me. I've been getting heroin out of this country for four years now, and never even the smell of a policeman—until now. Who would suspect nice Andy Jacobi, the man you love to ignore?' The bitterness seemed to fleck his lips like foam. 'You got on my nerves the other day, mooning over Zoltan like a lovesick schoolgirl. A beautiful chick like you—struck on him. I could see it in your eyes. He'd hypnotised you, dazzled you. It made me want to retch! That's why I said all those things to you on the balcony—to drop a little gall in the sweet cup of your adoration.'

'You're sick,' Rose said quietly. 'You're sick with jealousy and spite. Andy, for God's sake, let's go to the police. They'll understand, give you the help you need——'

'Are you kidding?' he crowed. 'Have you ever seen the inside of a Turkish jail? Forget it, kid. We're getting out of here.'

'Where are you taking me?' she asked.

'To the airport.'

'You'll never get away with it,' she said urgently.

'Think not?' He jerked the gun in his hand. 'With this stuck in your back, I'll get away with anything. We're going to stay real close, you and I. You'll enjoy that, won't you?' he sneered, glancing at her with hard, unblinking eyes. 'You're so stuck on Zoltan Stendhal that you haven't got eyes for anyone else. Well, maybe when we get to Morocco I'll change your mind for you. I'll show you that I'm also a man.'

'Morocco?' she quavered.

'That's right. I'm going to hold this gun against your spine, sweetheart. One slip, and I'll blow it all over the airport floor. You'll stay really close to me, and not say a word. We'll try and do it the quiet way. If there's any trouble, we'll show them exactly how things stand, won't we?'

'Supposing the police are waiting for you?' she said, her voice dry. 'Supposing they tackle you?'

'Then that'll be very bad news for you,' he said viciously. 'Because you'll be the first person to stop a bullet. But it won't come to that. We're going to walk into the terminal arm-in-arm, just like husband and wife. We're going to buy two tickets for the twelve noon flight to Casablanca, and go straight over to the departures lounge. And within an hour we ought to be airborne.'

'I haven't got a passport,' she lied desperately.

'Yes, you have,' he smiled thinly. 'I've got it with me. You and I are Mr and Mrs Holt, of Ankara. We're going on holiday. Got that?' He glanced at his wristwatch. 'That flight leaves in half an hour. With any luck, we'll be long gone before the first policeman puts two and two together, and comes looking for me.'

Rose sat, immobile, her hands clenched on her shoulder-bag.

'Cat got your tongue?' Andreas sneered. 'You didn't think I was capable of all this, did you? Well, I've got some surprises for you all. I'm capable of lots of things.' His leer was unmistakable in its meaning. 'And when we get to Morocco, beautiful Rose, I'm going to show you exactly what I'm capable of!'

CHAPTER NINE

THE airport terminal was crowded. Andreas walked Rose swiftly through the groups of people, his face blinking innocently. He had slung an overcoat over his right arm, and it concealed the pistol whose muzzle rested lightly against Rose's spine.

In a crazy way, she wasn't really frightened. Her hands were shaking, yes, and her knees were weak. But her inner joy overrode all that, giving her a confidence, an optimism that her situation far from warranted.

'This way,' Andy muttered, guiding her towards one of the airline booking offices with a twist of the gun in her back. Rose scarcely heard him. She was thanking God that Zoltan was free—free of the shadow that had hovered over him in her mind. God, she must have been crazy, crazy and blind! How could she, even for a second, have dreamed that Zoltan was a dealer in heroin? She had been overwrought, too susceptible to her own nerves. Maybe, in a way, she had actually *willed* this to happen. Willed it because her unconscious mind just couldn't accept the magnitude of what was happening to her, the fact that she was really falling in love.

Not the petty, sentimental feelings she had felt for Barry, but a mature, heart-wrenching, fully-developed love.

As they reached the airline counter, Andreas Jacobi rammed the pistol warningly against Rose's back. His expression of nervous kindliness didn't flicker as he did so.

'Two tickets to Casablanca, please,' he said. 'Here

are our passports.' He pushed the folder over with his left hand.

'Thank you, Mr——' The girl checked the passports. 'Mr Holt. Smoking or non-smoking?'

'Non-smoking—don't you think, dear?'

'Er—yes,' Rose agreed hastily as she felt the mouth of the gun press into her skin.

'Would you like a window seat, sir?'

'We'd like two seats on the aisle, please. And as close to the back of the aircraft as possible.'

'That's the noisiest area in this particular airplane,' the girl smiled. She looked at Rose. 'Your wife might like to sit further forward——'

'Just give us the seats we asked for,' Andy said sharply, his mask of kindliness slipping a bit. He was tense and frightened, and Rose could sense it in him. She knew that his finger was tight around the trigger of the gun, and her blood froze. The girl shrugged, turning to her computer.

'147 A and B,' she said. 'All right?'

'That's just fine,' Andy nodded. They waited in silence as the girl processed the tickets and filled them out. She glanced at her wristwatch.

'Your flight leaves in twenty minutes,' she informed them. 'Boarding is through Gate 5. Have a nice trip.'

'Thanks.' He slipped the tickets and the passports back into his pocket, and guided Rose along the crowded hall with the gun. 'Just act natural,' he commanded. 'Try and smile. And don't get any clever ideas, or you'll get an extra navel—in your back.'

'I'm starving,' she said, trying to keep her voice level. 'Can we have a cup of coffee?'

'What—so you can throw it in my face?' he sneered. 'Not a chance! We're just going to walk over to the departure lounge, and wait for that flight.' He looked at her, his eyes mean. 'Missing your boy-friend?'

'Yes,' she said calmly.

'Too bad. He'll be sweating blood when he realises I've got you with me. He really cares about you, doesn't he?'

'I think he does,' she replied quietly.

'And yet you were dumb enough to think he'd put that heroin in that head?' He chuckled. 'Shows you how clever I was. I never thought that stuff would be found—no one would dream of looking in a three-thousand-year-old sculpture. I was sure the reputation of the great Zoltan Stendhal would protect me. But having you denounce him to the police was quite a turn-up. What made you think he was the one?'

'I don't really know,' she confessed. 'Maybe the depth of my feelings for him actually blinded me. You see, I love him.'

'Love!' Andreas Jacobi sneered. 'What's lovable about that bastard?'

'He's a man,' she said in a low voice.

Andy's eyes narrowed viciously.

'Meaning I'm not?'

'You'll never be a hundredth of the man Zoltan is,' she said quietly.

'That's just earned you a little extra something when we reach Morocco,' he said, his face pale with anger.

'You think people ignore you because you're not brash and pushy,' she said, paying him no attention. 'Well, they don't. They ignore you because you're mean, and cruel, and small. You could never understand a man like Zoltan. You wouldn't in a million years understand the way I feel about him.'

'Shut up,' he said, his face tense. 'Open your mouth again, and I'll kill you. I swear it!'

But Rose ignored the cruel pressure of the gun in her back. She knew she had to distract Andy's attention. Had to prevent him from seeing Zoltan, who was striding towards them from the side, his face taut.

Be careful, my love, she prayed, he's got a gun!

'What led you into drug-dealing, Andy?' she asked steadily. 'Was it just the money? Or do you really enjoy the thought of all the suffering you cause at the other end?'

'I've warned you,' he muttered through gritted teeth. 'You'll pay for this in Casablanca!'

'Cheap threats,' she scorned, 'from a cheap little man.'

Andy's eyes narrowed, and Rose clenched her fists helplessly. Zoltan was almost within striking range of Andy now, waiting for the right moment.

'What's this all about?' Andy said suspiciously. 'You're up to something, you scheming little——' His sharp eyes raked the hall.

And as his eyes met Zoltan's, widening in shock, Zoltan sprang forward like a tiger. Rose gasped in pain as Zoltan's hard shoulder cannoned into her, knocking her away from Andy.

She spun round, aware of screams, just in time to see Zoltan's fist lash out and catch Andy a glancing blow on the temple. The little man sprawled backwards, his face a grimace of terror as he struggled to free the gun from his overcoat. Dimly, Rose was aware of two policemen darting forward, scattering appalled bystanders as they raised their submachine-guns.

But Zoltan himself had stumbled, and Andreas Jacobi was already on his feet, blood staining his face. He shouted something, Rose didn't catch what, and there was murder in his eyes. He raised the gun to point deliberately at Zoltan's face, and squeezed the trigger.

In that split second, Rose's mind snapped. With a gasp she threw herself between Zoltan and that wavering black muzzle, flinging her arms up to protect him. She heard Zoltan's warning, but it was too late.

There was terrifying noise that filled her ears, and a flash as bright as the sun.

And then she was spinning down a funnel as black and dense as night.

The harsh, haunting cry of the peacocks awoke her.

She stretched languidly in the bed, half opening her eyes to see the late afternoon sunlight flooding the room.

A mouth—she didn't have to guess whose—kissed her lips with gentle authority.

'Lie still a minute, my love—you're weak.'

'Oh, Zoltan!' She clung to his arms, trying to focus on his face. 'Are you all right? What happened?'

'You saved my life,' he smiled. 'That's what happened.'

'But the shot——'

'It went wide. You distracted Andreas' aim. But the muzzle-blast knocked you out. You've been asleep for about four hours.'

'Darling,' she whispered, her eyes wet, 'I'm so very, very sorry——'

His lips silenced her with efficient tenderness.

'Hush, my brave darling!' He cradled her in his arms, holding her close to his warmth. She shut her eyes in bliss, inhaling the sweet smell of his hair, his skin.

After a few minutes, the giddiness had faded, and Zoltan let her sit up in the bed. She was in the house in the Street of the Fountain, under the canopy of a huge double bed.

'I've finally managed to get you into my bedroom,' he said with quiet humour. 'How do you feel?'

'Fine,' she said, not letting go his hands. She stared into those unforgettable eyes, scarcely able to believe that he was still here, alive and well.

'What happened to Andy?' she whispered.

Zoltan's eyes darkened at the memory.

'If he had hurt a hair of your head, my sweet Rose, he would now be dead. When I saw him holding that gun to your back——' He clenched one fist, and stopped. 'The police disarmed him without having to fire a shot. He's being questioned at police headquarters right now.'

'Zoltan——' She shook her head, trying to find the words. 'I've been such a fool! God knows how I got it into my head that you'd put those drugs in that sculpture. It was Andy, in part. He was saying terrible things about you on the balcony that day——'

'I thought he might be,' Zoltan nodded grimly. 'Andreas Jacobi is a warped personality.'

'I know that now—but I didn't know it then. And the Moon card, the Tarot card that Sarai read for me—it got on my nerves. Oh, Zoltan,' she pleaded, throwing her arms around his neck, 'you must forgive me! I was overwrought, my mind was confused. Things had been happening so fast—and I was so very much in love with you——'

'Hush,' he smiled, rocking her in his arms. 'It was a perfectly natural conclusion to come to. What else could you think, except that I had hidden the heroin there? That was why I didn't want to take you down there that afternoon, you see—because I knew you'd spot the fake head.'

'You don't know how I felt, having to tell the police about it,' she said huskily. 'It nearly broke my heart to do it.'

'I would have thought the less of you if you hadn't,' he said quietly. 'By doing that—even though you loved me—you showed that you were the woman I thought you were. But you still warned me about it. Thank God you did!'

'I had to. I couldn't bear the thought of your going

to jail, Zoltan. I'd rather you escaped, even though I'd never see you again, than that you went to prison . . .'

He kissed her gently. 'It's you I feel sorry for,' he said, 'having to believe that I was a drug-smuggler.'

'It was terrible,' she smiled tremulously. 'Can you ever forgive me?'

'I don't have to forgive you, you sweet fool,' he smiled. 'You saved my life today at the risk of your own. There's very little I can say about that, Rose. My life is yours. It always has been.' He touched her face. 'There's so much you don't know, Rose. If you're feeling strong enough, let's walk in the garden and talk a while. But first, there's a panic-stricken surgeon in Chicago who's just dying to hear your voice. Come to the telephone.'

When she had phoned Freddie, her eyes still moist, she walked slowly out into the garden. He was waiting for her, a tall, magnificent figure in the golden light. She took the hand he offered her, and they wandered through the rhododendrons in the quiet air.

'Of course,' he told her, 'I knew about the heroin in that head. I found it two days before you did. You didn't know it, Rose, but you'd walked into the culmination of a very long operation involving Interpol and the Turkish police to track down a drug-smuggling gang. This wasn't the first consignment of heroin that Andreas Jacobi had tried to smuggle.'

'He told me he'd been dealing in drugs for four years,' she said. 'I thought he was so innocent, Zoltan. It was a shock to find out what he was really like.'

'He needs psychiatric help,' Zoltan nodded. 'He's a man consumed with hatred. Anyway, the police had narrowed their suspects down to a small group which included Andy. They'd had a tip-off that a large consignment was going to leave Turkey via the Middle Eastern Archaeology exhibition—and so, as soon as I got back from Agri, the drugs squad asked me if I would take on yet another undercover operation.' He smiled wryly. 'I'm no cloak-and-dagger man, Rose. To be quite frank, violence disgusts me. But I could hardly refuse. So I was appointed as director of the operation, and asked to try and track down the means by which the drugs were going to be sent. I didn't find the head until quite late—it was a brilliant idea.'

'A warped brilliance,' said Rose, and he nodded.

'Yes. And potentially very profitable. The police decided not to act. They wanted to wait until the drugs were picked up in New York by the other end of the operation—so that they could arrest the whole gang.'

'Oh,' said Rose in a small voice. 'And I've ruined everything, haven't I?'

'Not quite,' he chuckled. 'Andreas didn't get a chance to warn his partners in America—and the police are going to keep the news of his arrest secret until the pick-up is made in America. It should all go as planned. But, thank God, none of that concerns you or me now.'

'Zoltan,' she said, trembling, 'I don't think it had really sunk in until now—what it would have meant if you'd been a drug-smuggler——'

'It would have destroyed your love for me, for one thing,' he said absently. 'No one could love a man who dealt in such terrible things.' They stopped under a tangle of trees, the sunlight splashing them with gold. 'Why didn't you go to the police after you'd found that heroin? You'd have been safe there.'

'Instead I went to Andreas,' she said wryly, 'straight into the spider's web. I couldn't go to the police once I'd warned you that they were coming, Zoltan. I thought I'd be safe with Andy.' She smiled. 'And by what magic did you divine that I was with him?'

'Ah, that I cannot say,' he said, his eyes bright. 'I simply knew, that was all. When I got to your hotel and found you gone, some instinct told me where you had run to. From there, it was easy to work out what Andy's reaction would be—to get out of the country, holding you as his hostage.'

Rose stared up at him, adoring him. The sunlight made a mask of gold for his face, but now she knew what was behind that mask. The face of the man she loved, would always love.

'What a long way we've come,' Zoltan smiled, holding her close. 'Haven't we? From the snows of Agri, through the midnight waters of the Black Sea, to this precious moment of culmination.'

'In the Street of the Fountain,' she sighed. 'Why is it called that?'

'Four hundred years ago Mehmet Aga built a fountain here, to thank Allah for his good luck. It's still there, giving sweet water. I'll show it to you soon—when we are husband and wife.'

'Ah, my love,' she gasped, 'don't say that so lightly—it sends a pang right through my soul!'

'And do you think I'm impervious to such pangs?' he demanded. 'My soul, my beloved white doe, how I love you!'

His arms crushed her to him, his mouth taking hers with a passionate authority that shook her. Losing herself in the potent magic of his kiss, she melted against his body, her soft curves moulding themselves to his hardness. A thousand images flashed through her mind—Zoltan's fierce eyes in the snowstorm, his dizzying power against her in the water, the sensual smile on his mouth in the candlelight at the Garden House . . .

Images of the sweet past, promises of a sweeter future to come.

'You haven't said that you will marry me,' Zoltan said roughly, his eyes reflecting the fire that was burning inside him.

'You haven't asked,' she shuddered, clinging to his strength.

'Do I need to?'

'Just tell me that you love me, don't ever stop!'

'I love you,' he said, his voice warm velvet that brushed against her very heart, inflaming the bittersweet pain there at the same time as it soothed. 'I love you, love you . . .'

And the wind rustled through the rhododendron flowers, the only sound to disturb the deep peace of the evening.

Enter a uniquely exciting new world with

Harlequin American Romance™

Harlequin American Romances are the first romances to explore today's love relationships. These compelling novels reach into the hearts and minds of women across America... probing the most intimate moments of romance, love and desire.

You'll follow romantic heroines and irresistible men as they boldly face confusing choices. Career first, love later? Love without marriage? Long-distance relationships? All the experiences that make love real are captured in the tender, loving pages of **Harlequin American Romances.**

What makes American women so different when it comes to love? Find out with **Harlequin American Romance!**

Send for your introductory FREE book now!